'A delightful and varied collection of stories from all over Scotland. Theresa Breslin's style is so compelling and chatty that you feel she is sitting in the room with you, telling you her favourite tales of kelpies and brownies, talking birds, sheepdogs and selkies. And Kate Leiper's illustrations are stunning. This is a beautiful book, which will be treasured by children in Scotland and far afield.'

Julia Donaldson
CHILDREN'S LAUREATE

'This is a lovely book enhanced with the most beautiful illustrations. Folk stories have not lost their appeal in the modern world – it is books like this that will keep them alive.'

Alexander McCall Smith

granny told them stories every night before going to bed

it snorted and stamped its feet on the shingle shore

sparks flew from its hooves

I am the greatest bird because I can rise higher in the sky

selkies would dance and sing

seals swam in towards the shore

up and up the eagle soared

An Illustrated Treasury of

Scottish Folk and Fairy Tales

Theresa Breslin

Kate Leiper

Floris
Books

This book is for

Joanna Amy – T.B.

Iona – K.L.

First published in 2012 by Floris Books
Sixth printing 2016
Text © Theresa Breslin 2012
Illustrations © Kate Leiper 2012
Theresa Breslin and Kate Leiper have asserted their right
under the Copyright, Designs and Patent Act 1988
to be identified as the Author and Illustrator of this work.

The publisher acknowledges subsidy from Creative Scotland
towards the publication of this volume

British Library CIP data available
ISBN 978–086315–907–7

Printed in China through Asia Pacific Offset Ltd

Contents

they'd gobbled up the big bannock

e was caught fast and couldn't move

who jumped out of a pan

to run away as fast as I can

The Wee Bannock

This tale was told to me by my mother. It's a bit like the
story of the gingerbread man but with a happier outcome.
Selkirk, a town in the borders of Scotland, is especially
famous for its bannocks, which are more
like fruitcakes than the traditional oatmeal type
of bannock. They taste delicious.

There was once a guid-wife

who was married to a guid-man and their favourite thing to do was to eat lots of food.

One day the guid-wife decided to make some bannocks as a special treat.

"Mmmmm..." The guid-man rubbed his tummy. "I'm looking forward to this!" he said as he watched his wife bring out buttermilk, oatmeal, raisins and sultanas.

The guid-wife stirred the fruit, the oatmeal and the buttermilk all together. Next she rolled the mixture out until it was just the right thickness whereupon she shaped it into two big round bannocks.

Then she poured some fat into her cooking pan and set it on the fire. When it was sizzling hot she placed the two bannocks into the pan.

"Mmmmm..." The guid-wife rubbed *her* tummy. "What a wonderful sight!" she said as she watched the bannocks begin to turn toasty-roasty brown.

These two big bannocks were almost cooked when the guid-wife noticed that there was a small amount of the mixture left. Quickly she made this into a third, wee bannock. And she placed it in the pan beside the others.

Now the two big bannocks were ready so the guid-wife lifted them out of the pan and set them on two plates, one for her guid-man and one for herself. The guid-wife and her guid-man sat down to eat. In less than a minute they'd gobbled up the big bannocks for they both ate their food very fast indeed.

Then the guid-wife saw that the third wee bannock was toasty-roasty brown and she thought, "Oho! I'll have that wee bannock for myself." And she reached out her hand to lift the wee bannock from the pan.

But her guid-man had sniffed the air and smelled the lovely smell coming from the pan. And he thought to himself, "Oho! That's a bonnie wee bannock. I think I'll eat it up before anyone else does."

At the exact same moment the two of them made a grab for the wee bannock. The pan wobbled over the fire.

As the wee bannock slid to one side he glanced up and *he* thought, "Look at those two greedy folks. I've just seen them eat a whole big bannock each. They don't need a wee bannock like me."

So the wee bannock jumped out of the pan and skipped across the floor.

The guid-wife and the guid-man rushed to try to catch the wee bannock. *Wham!* They bumped into each other and fell over in a heap.

The wee bannock sang out as he scampered from the house:

I'm the wee bannock who
jumped out of a pan
To run away as fast as I can.

The wee bannock ran down the village street and he came to the cobbler's shop. Now the cobbler, a fat man, was working at his shop door. Bent over his last, he was nailing some new soles onto a pair of boots. He heard the commotion and raised his head.

When the cobbler spied the wee bannock running towards him he thought, "Oho! There's a bonnie wee bannock. I'd like to have a wee bannock like that for my breakfast!"

But the wee bannock had spied the cobbler and *he* thought, "The cobbler is well fed. He doesn't need a wee bannock like me."

So the wee bannock ran straight at the cobbler, and the cobbler fell back with his arms up. The boot he was holding flew into the air and came down and landed on his head.

And the wee bannock laughed as he ran away:

I'm the wee bannock who jumped out of a pan
To run away as fast as I can.
I left the guid-wife and the guid-man
And now I'm running away from thee
For you don't need a wee bannock like me!

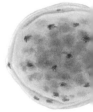

Further down the street a young girl was sitting at her window. She was winding a long skein of wool. When she saw the wee bannock she smacked her lips and thought, "Oho! I'd like to have a wee bannock to eat for my lunch."

She raced into the street and she tried to stop the wee bannock.

But the wee bannock saw her and thought, "There's a fine handsome lass. She doesn't need a wee bannock like me."

So the wee bannock dodged this way and that. Then he ran about in a circle – not two, but twenty times. The girl twisted round and round trying to follow the wee bannock. The more she turned, the more the wool tangled about her.

Soon she was caught fast and couldn't move.

The wee bannock laughed, and ran on, singing:

I'm the wee bannock who jumped out of a pan
To run away as fast as I can.
I left the guid-wife and the guid-man
And now I'm running away from thee
For you don't need a wee bannock like me!

At the end of the village was the smithy. The blacksmith was at his forge, hammering a horseshoe with a big hammer. When he saw the wee bannock running towards him he said, "Oho! There's a bonnie wee bannock. I could eat that wee bannock for my dinner."

13

But the wee bannock spotted the blacksmith and saw how big and strong the blacksmith was, and he thought, "The blacksmith doesn't need a wee bannock like me."

The blacksmith spread out his hands and legs to try to catch the wee bannock.

But the wee bannock ran between the blacksmith's legs, and he tripped him. The blacksmith dropped his hammer on his own toe and he hopped about squealing in pain.

And the wee bannock laughed and called back to him:

I'm the wee bannock who jumped out of a pan
To run away as fast as I can.
I left the guid-wife and the guid-man
And now I'm running away from thee
For you don't need a wee bannock like me!

And the wee bannock ran on out of the village towards the forest.

At the edge of the forest there were two poor children carrying a basket between them. They were collecting berries to eat for there was no food for them at home.

When the wee bannock saw the two hungry children, he thought, "Look at those two poor children. I'm sure they'd like a wee bannock to eat!"

And the wee bannock called out:

I'm the wee bannock who jumped out of a pan
To run away as fast as I can.
I left the guid-wife and the guid-man
I ran from the cobbler, the wool-winder, the smith
But I'll not run away from the likes of thee
For you folks do need a wee bannock like me!

So the wee bannock jumped into their basket. And they took him home, and that night the two poor children enjoyed a tasty wee bannock for their supper.

our fields will be ready for spring sowing

I have seen a fine black horse roaming there on the loch shore

no man can ride a kelpie and liv

smoke plumed from its nostrils

t snorted and stamped its feet on the shingle shore

sparks flew from its hooves

The Water Kelpie

This story is from the Highlands of Scotland, a land of
high mountains and mysterious glens where there are
many deep lochs. Some of the lochs are so deep,
it is said that if you throw a stone in the water it
will take a year and a day to hit the bottom.

Near the deep dark waters of Loch Ness

there lived a young lad by the name of Kyle. All the food the family had to eat was what they grew on the narrow strip of land between their cottage and the shores of the loch. Kyle had lived there quite happily for eleven years of his life helping his mother and father work their little croft when, one evening near the beginning of the year, he heard his mother speak to his father:

"It's almost time for spring sowing. You must rise early tomorrow and plough our fields to make them ready."

Kyle's father replied, "I am too old now to drag the plough around the fields and Kyle is still too young."

"What will happen to us then?" his mother asked in a worried voice. "If we do not plough our fields our crops will not grow and we will starve when winter comes."

Kyle's father pointed out the window. "I've seen a fine black horse roaming there on the loch shore these last nights of the silver moon. I think I could harness it and make it pull our plough."

"Oh no!" Kyle's mother said in alarm. "You mustn't go near that beast for it is one of the spirits that roam near fresh water to trap unwary folk and drown them. It isn't a horse. It is a water kelpie."

"Nonsense woman!" Her husband laughed. "That's a good strong horse. I can take the rope from our plough and tie it round thon horse's neck. I'll put my hands on its mane and haul myself onto its back and then I will tether it to our plough and it will do the work I cannot do. By this time tomorrow night our fields will be ready for spring sowing."

"I tell thee," Kyle's mother repeated, "that is not an ordinary horse. And it is said that a plain rope cannot control a kelpie, only a bridle made of iron can do that. Besides, the mane of the kelpie is said to be magic, so that if you try to grasp it your fingers become trapped, and also, anyone who mounts a kelpie becomes stuck to its back and cannot dismount." She took Kyle's father by the arm. "Husband," she begged, "do not go near the loch tonight."

But her husband wouldn't listen. He picked up the plough rope and, putting on his woollen plaid, he went out into the night.

Kyle's mother rushed to the door. "Husband, come back!" she cried. "The legend has been told in story and song that no man can tame the water kelpie of Loch Ness. Come back, husband! Come back or you will surely perish!"

But her husband had made up his mind. Kyle would have gone to help his father, for he was a brave boy, but his mother held on to him. They both watched from the doorway of their croft as Kyle's father approached the horse, which stood quietly beside the waters of the loch.

The horse didn't move as the rope was put around its neck. It remained very still as Kyle's father grasped its long mane and hauled himself up onto its back. But, as soon as the man was seated, a gleam of wickedness appeared in the horse's eyes.

"Look now!" Kyle's mother whispered in fear.

Suddenly the horse, which was indeed a water kelpie, seemed to grow in size until it was twice the height it had been before. It snorted and stamped its feet on the shingle shore so that sparks

22

flew from its hooves. Then the kelpie raised its great head and bared its teeth. Fire came from its throat and smoke plumed from its nostrils; it tossed its mane and its long hair turned to green serpents, which coiled and curled about the hands of the man. It reared up into the air, not once but three times. When its legs came crashing back to earth it began to race along the shoreline towards the deep waters of the loch.

"Jump off! Jump off!" Kyle's mother shouted to his father.

But the man couldn't jump off as his legs were stuck to the kelpie's side and his fingers were caught fast in its serpent mane. And the beast galloped into the waters of the loch and disappeared beneath the water.

Although Kyle and his mother searched and called out his father's name the whole night, the only answer they got was the howling of the wind and the dashing of the waves upon the rocks. The following morning the plough rope and the woollen plaid washed up on the shore.

Sadly Kyle brought them home to his mother who sat weeping by the fire. "Now we will surely starve to death," she lamented.

"I'll go to the loch," Kyle told her, "and catch some fish."

"There will be no fish in the waters where a kelpie lives," his mother replied.

"I can but try," said Kyle, and he went to the loch side and began to fish. He had sat there most of the day catching nothing when an old woman came by collecting firewood.

"A pleasant day," Kyle greeted her, "to be happy in the sun's warmth before it ends."

"That it is," the old woman said, "but I am not warm at night when my bones ache with the cold."

Now Kyle's father had often told him that no matter how poor you were there was always someone poorer. And so when Kyle saw that the old woman only had a worn shawl to keep her warm, he went to the cottage and brought out his father's woollen plaid for her.

"I do not take without giving in return," said the old woman, and she gave Kyle her worn shawl in exchange. She stared at him as she did, and she said, "It can be better to sit upon a plaidie than wrap it round you."

That day Kyle caught one fish.

The next day as Kyle was fishing the old woman came by again.

"Another fine day for you to enjoy," said Kyle.

"That it is," the old woman said, "although if I had bread in my stomach I would enjoy it more."

"Here, have mine," said Kyle, handing the old woman the bread his mother had given him for his breakfast.

"I do not take without giving in return," said the old woman, and she gave Kyle a lump of salt in a little pouch. She stared at him as she did, and she said, "Salt can be used to kill rather than to cure."

Kyle tied the pouch to the waistband of his trousers and that day he caught two fish.

On the third day when the old woman came by, Kyle wondered what she might want this time. He had given her his good plaid and his bread, what else did he have?

"A fair day," he said to her as she stopped to watch him fish. "Good for walking and talking."

"That it is," the old woman said, "but better it would be for me if I had a stout rope to pull my bucket from my well."

Kyle went and got the plough rope to give to her, for it was no use to him as he could not push the plough.

"I do not take without giving in return," said the old woman, and she handed Kyle a bridle for a horse. She stared at him as she did, and she said, "Iron is not only used to make a pot."

And that day Kyle caught three fish.

When his mother was cooking the fish for supper, Kyle told her about the old woman.

"She is well known hereabouts as a spae-wife," said his mother. "You mark well whatever she said to you and do not forget her words."

The days went past, and when the time for spring planting was almost gone there arrived another night when the moon shone silver. Kyle looked from the window of the croft and saw a black horse standing by the loch.

"The water kelpie!" he cried out.

His mother tried to distract him but Kyle was determined. "If we are to live this winter then we must plough the fields straight away. The only way to do it is if I can capture the kelpie and make it work for me."

"What makes you think you can succeed when your father failed?" his mother demanded. "The legend says no man can ride the water kelpie and live!"

But Kyle was determined to go. Although his mother barred the door, when she fell asleep he put the worn shawl around his shoulders and, taking the horse bridle, he climbed out of the window and went towards the loch.

"My but you are a bonnie beastie," Kyle murmured and he raised his hand to grasp the horse's mane so that he could haul himself upon its back. Then he paused and he remembered the words of the old woman when she had given him his first gift.

"It can be better to sit upon a plaidie than wrap it round you."

So Kyle took the shawl from his shoulders and spread it over the creature's back. Then he grabbed its mane and mounted the kelpie.

For a single second the beast stood still and then it swelled in size so that Kyle saw his cottage home become smaller and smaller and his mother, a tiny figure at the door, shrieking for him to jump off at once.

"I will not jump off," Kyle called out. "Not until the kelpie ploughs our fields."

When the kelpie heard this it snorted and tossed its head and it spoke in a terrible voice. "No man can ride a kelpie

and live. Now you are doomed as your father was before you, for I will not do as you command." Smoke and fire came from its mouth and it wrenched its head around to face the loch so that it could ride into the water and drown its rider.

Kyle leaned forward and gripped the mane more tightly. Beneath his fingers he felt the silky hair change to thick slimy green serpents. Spitting and hissing, the green snakes in the kelpie's mane tried to wind themselves around Kyle's hands, twist their way between his fingers and coil around his wrists.

And Kyle heard the words the old woman had spoken when she'd given him the second gift.

"Salt can be used to kill rather than to cure."

Quickly Kyle unloosed the little bag of salt at his waist and he crushed the lumps between his palms. At once the snakes shrank and withered so Kyle could grasp the kelpie's head and pull it the way he wanted it to go.

The kelpie was enraged and it thrashed out with its back legs three times and with its forelegs six times. Then the creature reared and plunged and tried to turn its head away from the land but Kyle held fast. He kept himself sitting on the old woman's plaid and didn't let his legs touch the back or the sides of the beast so that he wouldn't become stuck.

And Kyle recalled the words of the old woman when she had given him the third gift.

"Iron is not only used to make a pot."

He knew that the metal parts of the bridle were made of iron so he leaned down and slipped the bridle on and put the iron bit into the mouth of the kelpie. At once the beast quietened and became tame and would do what Kyle wanted.

Kyle trotted towards his croft and called to his mother to bring out their plough and to run and borrow a rope from their neighbour. This she did and Kyle harnessed the kelpie horse to the plough and led it up and down until all the fields were ploughed.

Not only did Kyle plough their own fields, he also ploughed the fields for miles around Loch Ness, for water kelpies have the strength of a hundred horses.

When the fields were done Kyle waited until the next silver moon then he led the kelpie to the water's edge. He slid the bit from its mouth and watched as the creature kicked up its heels and trotted into the water.

And that is the story of the water kelpie of Loch Ness, where the legend was true – for no man can master the water kelpie, but a boy did.

message and I will fly straight and sure

a swift and deadly prince of the skies

isle and gazed at his beloved

he would wait for her until the end of ti

he little bells tinkled one by one

The Goshawk and the Brave Lady

(from Sir Walter Scott's *Minstrelsy of the Scottish Borders*)

This is a story from the Scottish Borders. These were once known as the "Debatable Lands" when the Scots and the English would cross the Border to raid each other's houses and land. Many traditional tales of long ago involve the gallant hero rescuing the fragile maiden. In this story the heroine, Jean, decides to rescue herself.

Jean of Mortonhall was in love with William of Aikenwood

and William of Aikenwood was in love with Jean of Mortonhall. Good and well, you might say, but you would be wrong. For Aikenwood lay just north of the Border in the wild and beautiful countryside of bonny Scotland, while Mortonhall was a few miles south of the Border in the fair sweet land of England. And at the time of this story the English and the Scots did not get along together at all.

They ran off with each other's livestock and set fire to each other's castles and keeps. The Border reivers rode up and down the Border plundering and fighting and stealing sheep and cattle and generally behaving badly and causing trouble. Who was the most to blame was anyone's opinion, so I'll leave it up to yourself to be the judge of that.

Jean's father, the Earl of Mortonhall, had eight pretty daughters. He had warned them that *under no circumstances* were any one of them even to *smile* at a Scotsman, far less talk to one. Never in their lifetime would he allow them to visit Scotland, and he said that he would kill any Scotsman who entered through his gate.

This caused Jean, who was the youngest and prettiest, much distress and unhappiness. Many months previously, when riding out with her sisters, she had lost her way and wandered over the Border and into Aikenwood. She had stopped to let her horse drink at a little stream and there she had met William, a handsome young Scotsman. The two of them had at once fallen deeply in love.

William of Aikenwood was a fine hunter. He rode out each day with his hounds and his horses, his goshawk sitting proudly on the leather gauntlet on his left arm. Now this hawk had very special powers. As well as being a swift and deadly prince of the skies, it could think and talk almost as well as humans. Indeed, in some cases, better. And it wasn't long before the bonny bird noticed that its master was pining away.

"What ails thee, sire?" asked the clever goshawk. "I see that thy mind is not on the hunt today."

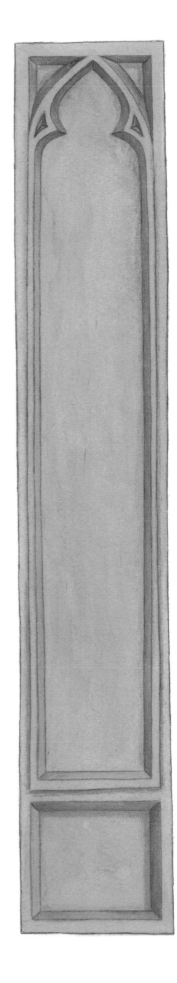

33

"That is true, my bonny bird," said William sadly. "Neither my mind nor my heart is with thee this morn. They are far, far away across the Border with my own dear Jean." He sighed heavily as he thought of how they could never be together. "I cannot even speak to her," he went on. "I am not allowed within sight of her, yet I want to tell her how much I dearly love her and wish to marry her."

The bird turned its bright black eyes on William and said, "Write out your message and I will fly straight and sure with it to thine own true love."

The lady Jean was sitting in her flower garden with her seven sisters when a strange bird came and settled in a nearby birch tree. Jean watched this bird as it began to sing. First, it sang sweet and low. Then it sang loud and clear. And as it sang Jean thought she heard it say her name over and over.

"Jean," trilled the bird,

Jeanie, Jeanie,
Fairest flower o' England, Jeanie,
Bend thy head and list to me
Jeanie, Jeanie, bonny Jeanie.

Jean stood up, left her sisters and came towards the branch where the bird sat.

"Why do you speak my name?" she asked, and she stretched out her hand.

The goshawk fluttered its feathers and William's message fell to the ground. Jean read his letter telling her that he would go each day to St Mary's Kirk near Aikenwood, where he wanted to marry her. He wrote that he hoped she would come to him and that he would wait for her until the end of time.

Jean thought for a while and then she smiled a merry smile.

"Tell your master I will be there," she said, "and that he must listen for the sound of bells."

Straightaway she went to see her father.

"Father," Jean spoke up bravely, "you would never allow me to spend my life in Scotland, but would you allow me to spend my death there?"

"Daughter," her father replied, "I do not understand your question."

"It is not a question that I ask of you," Jean replied, "but a boon that I beg. Grant me this wish. When I die I should like to be dressed in a linen shroud and carried forth upon a bier to rest in St Mary's Kirk."

Her father laughed loud and long. "I fear it is you who will be first to see me at rest," he said, "but if it pleases you, then I will grant you your wish."

Jean then spoke to her sisters. "If I should die," she said, "will you make me a shroud of finest cloth? Also, to mark my passing, I would like each of you to fasten a little silver bell upon it."

Her sisters tried to coax away her gloomy thoughts but finally they promised to do as Jean had asked them.

Jean hurried through the castle halls to her chamber. There she prepared a strong sleeping potion and drank it down. Her eyes closed, her cheeks turned pale and everyone thought she was dead.

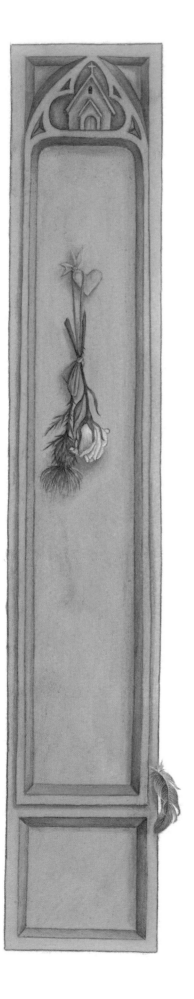

Her sisters came and stood over her. They could not rouse her. Then they lamented sorely at the loss of their youngest sister, but in keeping with her last wishes they sewed her a white linen shroud and each of them stitched a silver bell to the side.

The next morning they laid Jean on an oaken bier and carried her over the Border into Scotland towards Aikenwood. As the sad procession wound its way slowly to the Kirk of St Mary, all the little bells tinkled one by one, just as Jean had planned.

Deep in the surrounding forest, William of Aikenwood heard the bells ringing. He stretched out his arm and his faithful goshawk flew down to rest upon his wrist. Together they rode swiftly to St Mary's Kirk.

When the funeral party left, William slipped quietly into the tiny chapel. He strode down the aisle and gazed at his beloved Jean. Her face was as white as the lily flower and her cheek as cold as the snow on the Border hills. He knelt beside her and took her hand gently in his own. Then the rosy colour came back to her face and lips. She opened her eyes and smiled at her gallant.

"I am happy to be here with you, my love," said the Lady Jean.

"As I am with thee," said William of Aikenwood.

ran away down the road bawling

idled away his days in doing as little as possib

baby boy as he dribbled and drobbled goo over his clothes

I wish I had a little baby

verjoyed with this gift

Whuppity Stourie

This tale comes from the area of Galloway
in the Scottish Borders. It's very like
the tale of Rumpelstiltskin.

Between the River Esk
and the River Sark

in the lands of Galloway there was once a village called Kittlerumpit. Whether it's still there to this day is something you'll have to find out for yourself, for this story took place a long time ago when it was not unusual to meet one of the "Wee Folk" or the "Other People" as you went about your daily business.

Just outside this village of Kittlerumpit, in a small house at the edge of a big forest, lived a guid-wife and a guid-man. The guid-man was a happy-go-lucky sort of a person. Although he was a woodcutter and chopped and sold wood for a living, mainly he idled away his days in doing as little as possible, and amused himself of an evening by blethering to his neighbours. His guid-wife was quite the opposite sort of a person. She was hardworking and she cooked and cleaned and tended her garden and most importantly she looked after the fine fat pig they kept in a sty at the back of their house. Even though she worked hard and sang while she did so the guid-wife was not as happy as her guid-man. The reason for this was that the one thing that she wanted in all the world was a baby.

"Oh, I wish that I had a little baby," she would sigh as she tended her garden. "I would sit on a rug among the vegetables and flowers and my baby would fall asleep in my arms."

"Oh, I wish that I had a little baby," she would sigh as she cleaned her house. "I would sing a lullaby as I worked and my baby would smile as I did."

"Oh, I wish that I had a little baby," she would sigh as she cooked the dinner. "I would make tasty bannocks for my baby to eat."

The years passed and, one day, just as she was beginning to think that no baby was coming her way, a healthy little boy was born to the guid-wife and the guid-man.

The guid-wife was overjoyed with this gift of a baby and she wrapped him in a shawl and presented him to her husband.

"Look, my guid-man," she said. "Here is a happy, handsome, healthy boy for us to love and care for and look after."

After a few days of the baby being in the house the guid-man spoke to his wife. He wrinkled up his nose and he asked, "Doesn't this baby smell a bit?"

"Why, yes, husband!" answered the guid-wife. "That is a sign that our son is healthy. He fills his nappy at least twice a day."

After a few weeks of the baby being in the house the guid-man spoke to his wife. He rubbed his ears and complained. "Doesn't this baby make an awful lot of noise?"

"Why, yes, husband!" answered the guid-wife. "That is sign that our son is healthy. He has good strong lungs that he may cry out."

After a few months of the baby being in the house the guid-man spoke to his wife. He looked at the baby boy as he dribbled and drobbled goo over his clothes. "Doesn't this baby make an awful lot of mess?

"Why, yes, husband!" answered the guid-wife. "That is a sign that sharp white teeth are growing in his jaws and he'll be able to eat everything we can give him."

The guid-wife was delighted with her boy. But the guid-man was not so happy. Whereas before, his guid-wife did most of the work, now everything changed. The guid-wife cleaned the baby and fed the baby and rocked the baby to sleep. This meant that from early morning until late at night there were other tasks that needed to be done.

In the morning the guid-man had to rise early to gather firewood and light the fire.

In the afternoon the guid-man had to tend the garden.

In the evening the guid-man had to help make the dinner.

At night time the guid-man had to clear out the pigsty, for the big sow pig was getting ready to deliver a litter of piglets.

"I have to do this! I have to do that!" the guid-man moaned. "What happened to the times when I was left alone to do what I wanted? When I returned home after a tiring day spent chatting with my friends there used to be a nice warm meal on the table for me to eat. Now I have to make it for myself." And the guid-man longed for the times past when he could laze about doing nothing much all day. He took himself off to a corner of the house and he muttered to himself, "I don't think I'll stay here any longer."

When the next market day arrived, the guid-man pretended he had business to attend to and he bade his guid-wife farewell and he set off towards Kittlerumpit. But instead of going to the village he went on to the main road and resolved not to return home.

"I'll be better off away from this place," he said to himself. "I'll have time to stop and chat to whoever I want during the day and get a bit of peace to sleep at night. If I'm hungry I can pull a potato or a turnip from a field and I'll be well content on my own."

That night when her guid-man did not come home, the guid-wife went out into the road with a lantern and looked up and down to see if he was late returning from market.

48

She did the same thing the next night and the one after that, but there was no sign of her guid-man. Then she went into Kittlerumpit and asked here and there and everywhere at the neighbouring farms and cottages. Finally someone told her that they had seen her guid-man walking along the main road away from the village of Kittlerumpit saying loudly, "I'll have less work to do and more fresh air to breathe and peace and quiet on the open road than living in that house with a yelling, smelling baby."

The guid-wife was very sad when she realised that her husband was not coming back to her. But when she'd cried all the tears she could, she made up her mind to get on with her life as best she might.

She looked after her baby and he got bigger and more beautiful by the day and she thought him to be the bonniest baby in the Borders. She tended her little garden, and the flowers and the fruit and vegetables grew. And the fat sow pig got fatter and she knew that it would soon be time for the sow to have piglets. The guid-wife was very glad about this, for the little money that her husband had earned from woodcutting was nearly spent and she needed to be able to sell the piglets to have enough to live on.

However, one day when the guid-wife went to the sty behind the house the fat sow pig was lying down and would not get up.

The guid-wife prodded the pig with a stick but the pig stayed still.

The guid-wife threw cold water upon the pig but it would not move.

The guid-wife tried to tempt the pig with a fresh turnip but the pig did not budge.

The fat sow pig lay there with its eyes shut, its ears flat on its head and its legs bent beneath it. The guid-wife was very afraid for she knew that her pig was sick unto death and if the pig died then she and her baby would surely starve. She began to wail and weep and cry out and tear her hair.

"Oh, my pig, my fat sow pig!" the guid-wife lamented. "What will I do if you die? I will die and my baby will die too!"

And she sat down upon the ground and cried and cried and cried.

After a while she noticed in the distance a woman dressed in green coming along the road from the village of Kittlerumpit.

52

"What's the fuss about?" the woman in green asked when she drew nearer to the house. "What ails thee, guid-wife?"

"My pig," sobbed the guid-wife. "My fat sow pig is about to die. If she does then my baby and I will surely starve."

"Ah!" said the woman in green. Her voice quickened in interest. "You have a baby in the house?"

"I do," said the guid-wife. "Sleeping in his cradle is my handsome healthy boy. But he will be neither handsome nor healthy if the pig dies for I'll have no money to buy food for him."

A crafty look came into the eyes of the woman in green. "I might be able to help you. What would you give me if I was able to cure your fat sow pig?"

"Anything! Anything at all!" The guid-wife looked around her. "The flowers and fruit in my garden or the furniture in my house. I will give any of these to you."

The woman in green smiled a sly smile. "Anything at all?" she whispered softly. "You promise that I may have anything at all?"

And the guid-wife, never thinking for a minute that the woman in green had any wicked intent in her mind, promised that she had only to name the thing she wanted and it would be hers.

"Wait here," the woman in green told the guid-wife. She went into the sty and, taking some leaves of green myrtle from a bag she carried, she rubbed them over the eyes of the fat sow pig.

Suddenly the pig's eyes opened wide.

Then the woman in green took two mistletoe berries from a bag she carried and she placed one in each of the ears of the fat sow pig.

Suddenly the ears of the pig flapped up on its head.

Then the woman in green took some sprigs of heather from a bag she carried and she rubbed these on the legs of the fat sow pig.

Suddenly the pig's legs straightened out.

The fat sow pig grunted and rolled over and got to its feet and trundled about the pigsty.

"Thank you! Thank you, kind lady!" the guid-wife cried out in joy. "Now name the thing you want me to give you and it's yours."

The woman in green said nothing, but a horrible expression came onto her face. "What could the likes of you ever have that the likes of me might want?" she said nastily.

"I have a garden of beautiful flowers," said the guid-wife. "You may pick as many of them as you wish."

"All the flowers of the forest are mine already," said the woman in green in a terrible voice.

"I have many fine fruits," said the guid-wife. "They are yours to choose from."

"All the fruits of the fields are mine already," said the woman in green, again in a terrible voice.

"What about my furniture?" said the guid-wife.

"I could snatch all the furniture from your house with one sweep of my hand," said the woman in green in a more terrible voice.

"If not flowers, nor fruit, nor furniture, what can I possibly give you?" asked the guid-wife, beginning to be a little afraid.

"There's only one thing that the likes of you could have for the likes of me," said the woman in green in the most terrible voice yet. "What you have lies in the cradle in your house."

Upon hearing this, the guid-wife screamed. She realised that the person who stood before her was not, as she had thought, some kindly woman on the road who knew folk remedies for sick animals. The woman in green who had cured her pig was one of the Wee Folk and wanted to steal her baby from her.

No matter how the guid-wife pleaded and begged, the woman in green demanded the price they had agreed for her to cure the pig. Then the guid-wife remembered that any one of the Wee Folk who had tricked a human into handing over their baby could not come to claim the child until the evening of the third day. And even then they could not take the child if in that time the human managed to find out their name.

"No good it will do you," said the woman in green when the guid-wife told her this. "I'll be back at the end of three days and you must give me your baby."

The guid-wife was broken-hearted with grief, but she had always been a woman who tried to work her way out of a problem. Now she happed her baby up in a shawl and she went for a walk into the village of Kittlerumpit. But no one she spoke to there could help her in any way.

The next day the guid-wife happed her baby up in a shawl and she went for a walk along the banks of the river. But no one she met there could help her in any way.

On the third day the guid-wife happed her baby up in a shawl and she went for a walk into the forest. She walked and wandered further and further and then she felt so weary that she crawled into a thicket of bushes and lay down to sleep. When she woke up she saw the sun was beginning to go down and she was filled with despair.

"It is almost the end of the third day," she thought. "Soon the woman in green will come to my house and take my baby away."

All at once she heard singing. The guid-wife peered out of the bushes where she was hidden and she saw, walking along the forest path, the woman in green. The woman was singing a little song to herself, and the words of the song went like this:

Little kens the guid-wife at hame
That Whuppity Stourie is my name!

The guid-wife waited until the woman had passed by. Then she crept out of the thicket of bushes. Carrying her baby she ran swiftly by another way and got to her own house before the woman in green arrived.

When the woman in green demanded the price to be paid, the guid-wife again offered her the choice of fruits or flowers or furniture.

"I've told you already!" the woman in green screeched in fury. "There's only one thing that the likes of you could possibly have for the likes of me!" And she reached out her hand to take the human baby.

"There's one thing more that I have," replied the guid-wife of Kittlerumpit. "And the thing that I have is your own true name!"

And holding her baby tightly the guid-wife cried out in a loud voice:

I am the guid-wife who lives at hame
I know that Whuppity Stourie is your name!

At these words the woman in green jumped ninety-nine feet into the air and ran away down the road bawling.

So the guid-wife of Kittlerumpit kept her baby safe.

And I'm pleased also to tell you that not many weeks passed before the guid-man, who had become very hungry on the road eating only raw potatoes and turnips, realised that he missed, not just a warm meal, but also his guid-wife and his baby very much. He came back home again and resolved to work a bit harder than he had done before – though if he really did so is anybody's guess.

yowling and barking and paw...

a noise louder than thunder

...nfounded in the darkness

...uch a scrawny runt of a dog

a huge herd being guarded by one do...

The Shepherd's Dog

James Hogg was known as the Ettrick Shepherd because he worked near Ettrick in the Borders of Scotland. As well as being a shepherd he became a famous writer and although he lived over one hundred years ago his stories are still read today. He had many tales to tell of shepherds and of the dogs who helped them herd the sheep in their care. I've adapted these to tell the following story about one of his favourite sheepdogs in the shepherd's own words.

As I was a shepherd my dog was always my best friend.

When we were on the hills together I talked with my sheepdog all day. I shared every meal with him, and my plaid too when it rained.

One of my best dogs was named Sirrah. He was a good collie and a fine sheepdog.

But the first time I saw Sirrah he was far from being fine. A drover was dragging him along the road with a rope around his neck. He was half starved with his rib bones showing through his skin and his black coat matted and dirty.

"Why do you ill-use your collie dog so?" I asked the man, for I hated to see any animal badly treated.

"He is a useless cur," the drover replied, and he flicked the end of the rope over the dog's back.

The dog turned his head and snapped its teeth at the drover.

"See how bad tempered the beast is?" declared the drover. "Still he would bite me, though I've beaten him these last seven nights since I bought him."

I looked. But I did not see a bad-tempered beast. I saw an intelligent light in the dog's eyes and an animal whose spirit might be broken by cruelty.

"How much did you pay for him?" I asked the drover.

"Three shillings," he replied. "The worst three shillings I ever spent. I've kicked him and shouted at him and he will not obey me."

"But a dog should be treated with respect," I said.

"Respect!" the drover mocked me. "What! Would you have us call our animals Lord and Lady?"

"Perhaps neither Lord nor Lady," I replied. I knelt down before the poor forlorn beast. I could see then that the dog was really a pup, scarcely a year old. Imagine if one should treat a child in such a way! By slaps and cuffs. Was it any wonder the animal showed bad temper?"

"Take care," the drover said sourly. "He'll have your fingers off if you go near him."

"Well now," I spoke quietly to the dog. "What say you? Is there a title that you'd prefer? Not Lord nor Lady. How about Sir?"

The dog's ears went back, but he did not snarl at me. Perhaps he was surprised at being spoken to in a kinder voice than usual.

"Sirrah," I murmured even more softly. "Sirrah... yes, there's a name that would suit a dog like you."

The dog lay down, rested its head upon its paws and looked at me.

I spoke to the drover. "If you paid three shillings for him," I said, "I'll give you five."

"Nay," he answered smartly. "You'll give me a guinea. For I can see that you've taken a liking to him and I need recompense for all the food he's eaten since I got him and all the trouble he's caused me."

"The trouble was of your own making," I replied as smartly as he. "And by the looks of him you've fed him nothing but thin gruel. But I'll give you the guinea," I added at once, for I had indeed taken a strong liking to the dog and was now feared the drover would raise the price if I did not pay him quickly.

So I took the collie dog that I'd named Sirrah away from the drover. And the dog came with me quite readily, as if it knew that it had exchanged a bad master for a good friend.

But how my own human friends laughed when they heard I'd paid a whole guinea for such a scrawny runt of a dog.

"Twenty-one shillings!" one cried out. "That mangy cur is barely worth the three the drover paid for it!"

"It's a whelp," said another. "With that all-black coat and patch of brown upon its face, I'll wager it knows little of herding."

"Nor trained either," commented a third. "He's obviously never been taught to turn a sheep. Your flock will be scattered the length and breadth of the Borders."

"Pay them no heed," I told Sirrah as I set a bowl of warm food in front of him. "They're jealous that they have not got such a fine dog."

My fellow shepherds were right about one thing, Sirrah *was* untrained. But being young meant that he was eager to learn. And I was proved right about the intelligent gleam I had spotted in my dog's eyes. For when I took him on the hill with an older dog and began to teach him how to become a dog fit for herding sheep, Sirrah picked up the idea of what I wanted right away. I held him fast by the collar and spoke to him quietly as I set the older dog the task of herding a number of sheep into a small pen fold I'd erected for the purpose upon some pasture land.

"Do you see?" I asked Sirrah. "Do you see now what happens when I call out like this, 'Hey up! Hey up!'"

And I waited while the older dog rounded up the sheep into a tight bunch.

"Now watch, Sirrah," I said, "as to what that dog does when I raise my stick and point." Within a minute or so the older dog had these sheep inside the pen.

I had chosen younger and therefore more biddable sheep for this training purpose but, even so, sheep do sense when a dog is inexperienced and are always ready to take advantage. But with Sirrah, before the afternoon was out he had mastered the basic principle of herding and I knew that it wouldn't be long before he learned the whistles and other calls I used.

By the time lambing season arrived, Sirrah was a full working sheepdog and the other shepherds saw that I had won his trust and he and I were suited to each other. They had to admit that they'd been wrong about his capabilities.

There was, however, one aspect of Sirrah where he had no talent whatsoever and that was his ear for music. This wouldn't have been anything to trouble me with had he merely ignored people singing, or retired to a quiet corner when this happened – as most other dogs might. But I do believe that Sirrah actually liked music. The farmer of the farm I worked in at the time called his family to prayer and hymn-singing morning and evening. By morning I was usually out in the fields or on the hills, and by evening, often being bone-weary, I was asleep in the byre-loft while Sirrah rested in the hay-nook in a corner below. But the kitchen was a short distance from where we slept and as soon as Sirrah heard the opening lines of the psalm he fell to yowling and barking and pawing at the door that he might get out and join the congregation.

This in itself was well-enough contained for I kept the barn door firmly latched. Therefore those at prayers in the kitchen were unaware that they had another who was keen to join them. But it happened that one Sunday as I went to the kirk in Ettrick that the door of the barn was not properly closed. On finding himself free, being a faithful dog, Sirrah followed me to my place of worship. And was that not the very morning the minister of the parish decided he would choose me to lead the hymn singing? And did it not happen that as I stood up there before the congregation I espied from the window a black streak of running dog coming fast over the hill towards the kirk?

A tremor went through me for I knew what would happen. As I lifted the book I saw a familiar canine face appear round the door of the kirk, and then my four-footed friend took up a position, sitting erect, tongue hanging out, in the middle of the aisle. The moment my voice struck up the psalm with "might and majesty", Sirrah joined in with great gusto. There was nothing for it but to carry on as best I might, but the louder I sang the louder my dog yowled. The older folks coughed and spluttered into their handker-chiefs. The girls pulled down the brims of their bonnets and bit their lips as their cheeks glowed red with the effort of trying not to giggle. And the shepherds bent their foreheads to rest on the pew in front of them to pretend they were praying. They tried to muffle the sound of their laughter by burying their faces in their plaids but their snorts and guffaws of mirth shook the rafters of the church.

And I was never asked to lead the hymn singing again in Ettrick Kirk.

Despite the unmusical side of his nature, Sirrah went on to develop a most obliging trait in his temperament. I think this was due to the fact that he recalled his earlier harsh life and was grateful to me for rescuing him from it. This was never proved so much as when we had the episode of the lost lambs.

After lambing there comes a time when the young lambs have to be weaned from their mothers. And on this occasion several shepherds including myself had charge of gathering up seven hundred lambs. These were short-faced lambs of a difficult and contrary breed of sheep and it had taken us two whole days and unto the evening of the third to bring them in. As darkness fell, we all were settled and so we lit our fires and set ourselves to watch over them throughout the night.

Suddenly they broke loose and the whole herd began to race up the moor towards us. The sound of their running made a noise louder than thunder

"Sirrah!" I cried. "My dog, Sirrah! The lambs are running! The lambs are running!"

The shepherds leapt to their feet. We took off our plaids and we shook them out before us. We waved and flapped but still the lambs came on at us. We raised our arms and circled the plaids above our heads and created a great hullabaloo.

And again I shouted out for my dog, not really believing but still hoping he might hear me above the din.

"Sirrah!" I shouted. "Hey up! Sirrah! Hey up!"

We shepherds yelled and stamped our feet. Spreading our arms wide we crouched down that we might capture a few. But these bold short-faced lambs ran and leapt among us sprightly and swift, and dainty on their feet to trip along where we could not go. And we were confounded in the darkness and tumbled over each other and only succeeded in splitting the herd so that one lot ran north and the other to the east.

We snatched brands from our fires and we traipsed about those hills, north and east, and south and west. We found not a single lamb. Our brands burned down and the fires went out and we came home, for there was nothing else we could do.

By the pale light of the pearly dawn the dogs came home too; tails between their legs, they slunk in. One by one they came, with nothing except bewildered looks upon their faces as if they too could scarce believe that they had lost every lamb from the flock.

But one dog did not come home.

Sirrah.

I whistled and I called. And I went up the glen road and back, but there was no sign. With my hand I shaded my eyes against the bright sun now rising in the sky. But no Sirrah could I see.

"We must tell the farmer what has happened," said one of the shepherds. "Let him know there are many more days work to be done now. All farmhands need to come along and fan out across the hills to search for the lambs and see how many we are able to find."

But now I was uneasy as to the whereabouts of Sirrah. He was a resourceful dog and I began to fear that some ill had happened to him. There were a few deep ravines and one gorge in particular near the Great Cleuch where the edge was unsafe and crumbled away, and a man or beast being unwary might fall and smash upon the rocks below, and lie there and never be found.

The shepherds got ready to go to the farmer and say we had not lost a few, nor a dozen, nor a score of his lambs, but every single one. All seven hundred lambs bolted and disappeared into the vast darkness of the night, swallowed up among the glens and heaven knows what happened to them.

"You must do what you must do," I told them. "What I must do is search for my dog, Sirrah."

I got up and wrapped my plaid around me and took my staff in one hand.

One of the other men got up and said, "I will do it. I will go and speak to the farmer."

"Bide your time," the oldest shepherd there told this man. "For although I also was one of those who doubted the talents of the dog, Sirrah, I think that we should wait until his owner has at least tried to recover his body."

I left the group of men and went away towards the Great Cleuch. There was no trace of Sirrah or indeed any lambs there, though if any had sought shelter then that was the place they would have gone.

With a heavy heart I walked the three miles to the gorge.

73

The sun was fully up now as I approached the gorge. Most carefully, by getting down on all fours, I stretched the full length of my body out flat to peer over the edge and down into the depths of the ravine. In fear and trembling I looked, terrified that I might see the broken body of my beloved dog.

But a wondrous sight met my eyes. Far below me was a great assembly of lambs; a huge herd being guarded by one dog, Sirrah.

"Sirrah!" I couldn't help myself. I cried out in joy and found tears upon my cheeks.

And there he stayed while I scrambled down by a most difficult path. I saw Sirrah, standing true to his charge with not one lamb missing.

How had he collected them in the dark as they had broken and run in different directions? How had he the wit to gather them in the deep narrow ravine where they'd little chance to escape? How had he found them a safe passage to the floor of the gorge that they might go down without injury? I have been a shepherd many years but this I cannot answer.

All I know is that there was only one dog capable of doing this.
My dog, Sirrah.

have a dress made of gold

marry for love and not for mon

every girl in his father's kingdo

nippit fit and dippit fit behind the k

what an unusual pair of shoes

Rashie Coat

The fairy folk of Scotland were often called the "Wee Folk" or the "Other People" and were thought to dress in green when they took human form. They could be very unkind to humans but usually a fairy that had chosen to live in a house or castle was kind and helpful, like this one in the Scottish version of the story of Cinderella.

There was once a king of a small kingdom

and this king was not very rich. Although he was poor the king was cunning, and he thought of a way that he might have more money. He had one child, a bonny daughter, and he made up his mind that he would marry her to the richest man in his kingdom. One day he called his daughter to him and told her that she must marry the rich man. But his daughter did not like this man, for it was well known that the rich man was proud and also cruel to his servants and ill-treated the animals in his care.

"I will not marry this man," the girl told her father, the king.

"Why ever not?" demanded her father.

Now, as well as being very pretty, the king's daughter was a good and sensible girl, and long ago she had made up *her* mind that she would only marry for love and not for money. But she knew that she couldn't say this to her father as he would not understand, so she only repeated what she had said: "I will not marry this man."

80

"You will marry him," her father said sternly. "I am your father and I am the king and you must do as I say. I will call for you tomorrow and you must give me a different answer."

The girl knew that she would have to think of a reason to stop her father making her marry. She went to the hen-wife who lived on the hill and asked, "What can I do? I do not want to marry a man I do not love. What can I do?"

"A bride-to-be may ask for three gifts from the man she is to marry," the hen-wife told her. "You must ask for a gift from this man. Ask for something that he cannot give you."

The girl thought for one minute. "I'll ask for a gowden gown," she said. "For no one can make a dress from gold."

When her father, the king, called her the next day, the girl said to him, "If this man wishes to marry me then he must give me a gowden gown."

"That's impossible!" exclaimed the king. "How can anyone make a dress from gold?"

"I do not know," replied the girl, "but that is what I want."

The king went and spoke to the rich man and told him that his daughter wanted a gift of a gowden gown. The rich man thought very hard about what he could do. He dearly wanted to marry the king's daughter for he knew that a king's daughter is a princess and if he married her then he would become a prince. And, as he was a proud man, he wanted very much to be a prince and to have people bow down before him. He called his wisest men and his best dressmakers and together they found a way to make cloth from gold, and they made a golden dress for the king's daughter.

Many a girl would be pleased to have a dress made of gold but not the king's daughter. She ran again to the hen-wife who lived on the hill and cried out, "What can I do? The rich man has given me a gowden gown as I asked, but I do not want to marry a man I do not love. What can I do?"

"You must ask for a second gift," said the hen-wife. "Ask for something that he cannot give you."

Then the girl thought for two minutes. "I'll ask for shoon made from the feathers of wild birds," she said. "For no one can gather enough feathers from the wild birds to make a pair of shoes."

The girl went back to her father and told him that she wanted a second gift of wild-bird-feather shoon.

"That's impossible!" exclaimed the king. "How can anyone make shoes from wild bird feathers?"

"I do not know," replied the girl, "but that is what I want."

The king went and spoke to the rich man and told him that his daughter wanted a pair of shoes made from the feathers of wild birds. The rich man thought very hard about what he could do. He dearly wanted to marry the king's daughter for he thought that as soon as they were married he would have lots more servants to rule over and be cruel to. The rich man called his wisest men and his best shoemakers together. His wise men told him to scatter bread-crumbs around his courtyard and when the wild birds flew down to eat, he would be able to catch them in nets. This he did, and the rich man had his servants pluck the feathers from the wild birds as they tried to escape. When the king's daughter heard the noise and the screeching of the trapped birds she came and lifted the

corners of the nets so that the birds could escape, for she hated to see any wild creature being hurt. But the rich man already had enough feathers for his purpose. And, as the birds flew away to freedom in the deep woods, his shoemakers glued and shaped the feathers to make a pair of shoes for the king's daughter.

Many a girl would be pleased to have such an unusual pair of shoes made from the feathers of wild birds, but not the king's daughter. She ran again to the hen-wife who lived on the hill and cried out. "What can I do? The rich man has given me wild-bird-feather shoon as I asked, but I do not want to marry a man I do not love. What can I do?"

"You must ask for a third gift," said the hen-wife. "Ask for something that he cannot give you. But be warned," the hen-wife added, "for this will be your third and last gift and you can ask for no more. If he gives you this gift then you will have to marry the rich man."

This time the girl thought for three minutes. "I'll ask for a coat made from the rashies that grow by the river," she said. "And I will tell him that this will be the coat I will wear on our wedding day. Even if he is able to make a coat from rashies, this rich man is so proud that he will not want a bride who would wear such a cheap coat to stand beside her husband on their wedding day."

The girl went back to her father and told him that she wanted a third gift of a rashie coat.

"That's impossible!" exclaimed the king. "How can anyone make a coat from rushes?"

"I do not know," replied the girl, "but that is what I want. And tell him I will wear it on my wedding day."

"This is you third and last gift," her father said sternly. "If the rich man gives you this you must marry him."

The king went and spoke to the rich man and told him that his daughter wanted a coat made from rashies and that she intended to wear it as her bridal outfit. The rich man thought very hard about what he could do. He dearly wanted to marry the king's daughter, even though he saw that she had a mind of her own and it would not be easy to govern her. But he thought, as soon as they were married he would get rid of the king and he would become king of the kingdom and rule over everyone including his wife. So the rich man called his wisest men and his best weavers together. His wise men told him to cut down the rushes when they were soft and pliant, and then his weavers made a special loom and they wove a rashie coat for the king's daughter.

Now not very many girls would be pleased to have a coat made from the green and brown rushes from the river, but the king's daughter thought it the most beautiful coat she'd ever seen. But she wept bitter tears as she put it on for she did not want to wear it as a bridal outfit to be married to the rich man.

Her father spoke to her: "We have wasted enough time. The wedding will take place tomorrow. The rich man has said you have to wear your gown of gold under your rashie coat and, as soon as you are married, he will take away the rashie coat and burn it. Then everyone will see your golden gown, which is a proper dress to wear as his bride. As he will be your husband you will have to do as he wishes."

The king's daughter said nothing but she thought to herself, "I will not marry a man I do not love."

That night she wrapped up her gowden gown and her bird-feather shoon and her rashie coat and she crept out of the palace. She ran away over the hill, past the house of the hen-wife, through the deep woods and into the next kingdom. She had no money and she was very hungry, and so she went to one of the castles belonging to the king of that kingdom and she knocked on the kitchen door and asked, "Have you any work that I might do in exchange for something to eat and somewhere to rest my head at night?"

The cook took pity on her and he pointed to a huge pile of pots and pans. "There," he said, "you may scour and scrub those every day until they're shining bright, and among them is where you may rest your head at night."

So the king's daughter scrubbed and scoured until the pots and pans shone brightly. And at night she laid down upon her gowden gown and, with her bird-feather shoon as a pillow and her rashie coat as a blanket, she slept until morning.

The days passed in this way until Sunday arrived and everyone in the castle got ready to go to the kirk.

"We are all going to church," the cook told the girl. "I have put oatmeal in a big cauldron on the fire to make porridge. You must stand behind the cauldron and watch it until we get back and keep stirring the porridge to stop it from burning."

Now the king's daughter was a good girl and she wanted to go to the kirk on Sunday too.

"How can I go to church?" she wondered aloud. "If I do, then the porridge will burn and I will be sent away from here."

At that moment a lady dressed in green appeared in the kitchen. The girl knew at once that this lady was one of the Wee Folk and that if she had chosen to stay in the castle then she must be a kindly house fairy.

"You can go to the kirk," said the house fairy, "and I will stir the porridge for you while you are at church."

The king's daughter's clothes were stained with all the work she'd been doing in the kitchen so she quickly slipped on her gowden gown and she ran off happily to the kirk.

Now the king of this second kingdom had a son, a young and handsome prince, who was also at the kirk that morning. As soon as the prince spied the first king's daughter coming into the church his eyes opened wide. He was dazzled by the glow from her golden gown but he was more dazzled by the rosy cheeks and the pretty appearance of the girl's face.

"Who is that bonny girl?" he asked his pageboy and the lords and ladies who had come with him to church. They shook their heads for they didn't know.

When the service ended the prince looked around for the bonny girl but she had gone. She had run back to the castle as fast as she could so that when the cook came into the kitchen she was standing behind the cauldron stirring the porridge as he'd told her to.

All through the week the girl worked at keeping the pots and pans clean and at night she slept among them. She was happy enough doing this until the following Sunday when she was asked to wait behind to stir the porridge while everyone else went to the kirk.

"I'd rather be at the kirk," she said aloud. "I do wish that someone else would mind the cauldron of porridge while I go to say my prayers."

The good fairy of the house appeared once more. "I will stir the porridge," she said, "and stop it burning until you return."

Now the weather was a little colder this week so, as well as changing into her gowden gown, the girl decided to put on her shoon made of wild bird feathers and she ran off happily to the kirk.

The prince was sitting in his place as the girl came into the church and at once he saw the gleam of the gowden gown and he also heard the rustle of the bird-feather shoon.

"What an unusual pair of shoes!" he thought as he spied the bird-feather shoon. "And what an unusual girl too," he marvelled as he watched her say her prayers – for most of the other girls whispered and giggled with each other while they were in church. But although the prince hurried outside quickly after the service, by the time he did so the bonny girl had gone. He resolved that next

Sunday he would wait by the door and that way he would be able to stop the girl before she disappeared.

When the next Sunday arrived, the good fairy of the house appeared again in the kitchen to help the girl so that she could go to church. The girl put on her gowden gown, she put on her bird-feather shoon and, as the weather was now even colder, she decided to put on her rashie coat. And she ran off happily to the kirk.

When the girl entered through the door the heart of the king's son began to beat faster. "Why!" he exclaimed. "Even when she wears a cheap plain coat made from river rushes I can still see her goodness and beauty. I do believe I have fallen in love with this bonny girl. I *must* speak to her today."

As soon as the service was over the girl left the church. The king's son leapt up and ran after her.

"Wait!" he cried out.

The girl looked over her shoulder. She saw a man chasing her with a pageboy and some lords and ladies following him. The girl was afraid. "They want to catch me and take me back to my father," she thought. So she began to hurry along the road.

"Come back!" the prince shouted. "Come back! Girl with the rashie coat! Please wait! I want to talk to you!"

But the girl started to run. She went faster and faster. So much so that she tripped and fell, but she got up and ran on. As she disappeared round a bend the prince stopped and looked down at the road. When the girl had tripped, one of her bird-feather shoon had come off. The prince bent down. He lifted the shoe made from wild bird feathers and he held it up.

"I will marry the girl known as Rashie Coat," he declared. "And I will be able to find out who she is, for I will make every girl in the kingdom try on this shoe. The girl whose foot fits inside the shoe will be my wife."

Now very, very many girls came and tried on the bird-feather shoe, but not one of their feet fitted inside. They were either too big or too small.

The prince was in despair for he thought that every girl in his father's kingdom had tried on the shoe. He didn't know that the girl he sought was the one who stood behind the cauldron of porridge and washed the pots and pans in the castle kitchen, and that she was too frightened to come out.

But the hen-wife who lived on the hill heard of the search taking place in the kingdom nearby and guessed what was happening.

"Aha!" she thought. "I know who the person is who owns a pair of shoon made from the feathers of wild birds! The daughter of the king of this kingdom must be too frightened to come forward in case she is sent back here to marry the rich man. But I have a daughter and I'd very much like for her to marry a king's son." So the hen-wife took her own daughter to the next kingdom and she presented her to try on the shoe made from bird feathers.

Now the foot of the hen-wife's daughter was too big to fit into the bird-feather shoe. But before the pageboy who was holding the shoe could say anything the hen-wife snatched the shoe from his hand.

"Let me try," she said and she pushed the toes of her daughter's foot into the top of the shoe.

"But her toes are too long," said the pageboy.

"No more they are," said the hen-wife. She stealthily took a pair of scissors from the pocket of her apron and cruelly she clippit and clippit the toes of her daughter.

"There!" she said. "My daughter's toes are a clippit fit into the bird-feather shoe."

"But her heel is too broad," said the pageboy.

"No more it is," said the hen-wife, and she pressed and pinched and squeezed until her daughter's heel was a nippit fit in the back of the shoe.

And so, by clippit and nippit, and by nippit and clippit, the hen-wife made her daughter's foot fit in the bird-feather shoe.

Now the hen-wife had also coloured and styled her daughter's hair to be the same as the first king's daughter and she had powdered and painted her face to make her have the same rosy cheeks as Rashie Coat. So the prince believed that this indeed was the girl he had seen in the kirk on a Sunday.

The prince said to the hen-wife's daughter, "Climb on the back of my horse and I will take you to my father at his palace, for he should meet the girl I want to marry."

So the daughter of the hen-wife climbed up on the prince's horse and off they rode.

The way they went took them through the deep woods. Now the wild birds who fly everywhere had heard what was happening in the kingdom and they remembered that it was the girl now known as Rashie Coat that had rescued them from the nets of the rich man. So when they saw the prince galloping through the deep woods with the hen-wife's daughter on the back of his horse, they came down from their nests in the trees and they flew about his head and they chirruped and they sang a song:

Nippit fit and clippit fit
Behind the king's son rides
But bonny fit and pretty fit
Behind the cauldron hides.

The prince drew rein on his horse and he asked the hen-wife's daughter what this meant. The poor girl burst into tears and told him what her mother had done. At once the prince took the bird-feather shoe from her foot and saw the terrible state of the girl's toes and heels. He turned his horse around and set off back to the castle, and when he got there he went straight to the kitchen.

There, behind the big porridge cauldron he found Rashie Coat. The prince was happy to find his true love and when Rashie Coat realised that the prince was a good man and that he loved her for herself, she fell in love with him too.

And so they were married, so that the girl who had decided she would marry for love did just that. On her wedding day the king's daughter wore her bird-feather shoon, her gowden gown, and on top of that she wore her rashie coat.

sealskin caught up in the rock

seals swam in towards the shore

selkies would dance and sing

y seashell on the empty pillow

footprints marked the sand from seashore to cottage

The Selkie of Sanday

The Orkney Islands lie north of the mainland of Scotland. All around their shores are reefs and large rocks known as skerries where the waters of the North Sea and the Atlantic Ocean meet and mingle. Here, seals, or "selkies" as they are often called, can be seen swimming or basking on the rocks. It's thought that at certain times a selkie can take off its skin and become human. There are many stories about selkies in Scottish folklore. This one is my own.

Magnus was a fisherman who lived alone in a cottage

by the edge of a bay on the Orkney Island of Sanday. He often wished that he could meet a nice girl with whom he might share his life.

"How pleasant it would be," he thought, "to have someone to walk with me along the seashore on a summer's evening. We'd hold hands and watch the light sparkle on the waves, for at Midsummer here the sun never really goes down. And, during the cold dark winter, we'd sit snug and warm in front of our fire."

But Magnus was shy, and anytime he met a girl he'd no idea what to say to her. Besides which, he was only a poor fisherman and had little to offer any girl to persuade her to become his wife. So he resigned himself to being on his own, and each day he sailed his boat out into the bay to catch fish that he might have something to cook for his supper.

One summer evening – when daylight does not fade into dark night in the north, but stretches through, and the sun stays in the

sky even after midnight – the fishing became very bad. From the beginning of June Magnus went out to fish and caught nothing. As the days went on Magnus noticed that there were many more seals in the water. He'd heard tales about the seal people and how they gathered together at Midsummer. The older folks of Sanday claimed to have seen selkies swim onto the beach at this time of year and slide off their scalskins to take the form of humans: men, women and children. Then the selkies would dance and sing through the long, long Midsummer's Eve.

"That's why there are no fish in the bay," Magnus said to himself. "The selkies have chosen this spot to gather for Midsummer. They are eating the fish and there is none left for me."

The next day, which was Midsummer's Eve, Magnus resolved to take his boat further out to the skerries that lay beyond the bay.  He moored near to one of these small rocky islands to fish. Magnus had no more luck that day than any other, and so, in the late evening, sad and hungry, he set sail for home. As he came back into the bay he saw the most wondrous sight. All along the shoreline the selkies in human form were splashing and skipping in the water. Across the sea floated the sound of their singing, mournful yet beautiful, low and rhythmic, like the murmur of waves lapping on the beach.

"Ah!" Magnus spoke softly, his hunger forgotten as he watched the magical creatures.

Suddenly the sky darkened. Great storm clouds puffed up and glowered down from above. The wind changed and a huge breaker came roiling and boiling in from the open water. At once the selkies left

off their games and dashed to gather their sealskins and slip them on. Within minutes they were gone from the beach. Just in time! The enormous wave crashed against the shore, sending spray flying. Water thundered over the rocks.

Magnus struggled to keep his boat afloat. When he'd weathered the storm and made it to shore, the beach was deserted. Tired and weary he went to bed and fell asleep.

In the early part of the night Magnus awoke. He thought he'd heard a cry, a thin reedy sound. "It's a seabird," he decided, "a mother looking for a lost chick." And so he went back to sleep.

He was wakened in the middle of the night by a moaning noise. "That's the run of the tide going through the skerries," Magnus thought, and once more he fell asleep.

But when Magnus arose early the next morning, still he could hear a plaintive wailing, rising and falling in the air.

It was not the cry of a gull nor the sea funnelling through the rock channels. It was a human voice, echoing a lament across the water. Magnus got into his boat and set out in the direction of the noise. On the furthest skerry of the bay crouched a young woman with long hair, which curled and coiled about her body. She was shivering with cold. Magnus picked up the old blanket that he kept in the bottom of his boat and he threw it to her to wrap herself in. He brought the boat close to the rock, reached out his hands and pulled her aboard.

Now that he was nearer to the girl, Magnus could see that, although her eyes were a troubled cloudy grey like the colour of a stormy sea, she was beautiful in a strange and different way from ordinary girls. He rowed ashore and led her to his cottage where she lay down to rest.

As she slept Magnus took the boat out again, for he'd heard stories of the selkies, and how it sometimes happened that they could lose their selkie skin. He sailed in and out of the skerries and, sure enough, there was a sealskin caught up in the rocks at the end of the bay.

When Magnus came home he opened his cottage door carefully and quietly and looked at the sleeping girl. Now, he should really have woken her and given the girl her sealskin so that she could put it on and return to her family in the sea. But as he heard her breath rise and fall and saw her bonny face, Magnus fell deeply in love with her.

So Magnus pulled an old chest out from under the bed and he hid the sealskin at the bottom. Then he locked it up and pushed it far under the bed. He warmed some oatmeal and as he did the girl awoke. Magnus tried to speak to the selkie-girl but she wouldn't answer. When he offered her a bowl of oatmeal she shook her head. He knew that she must be hungry but as he approached her with the food she shrank away from him.

Suddenly Magnus recalled another thing that the old folk of Sanday said about the selkies – they loved music. He took down his fiddle from above the mantelshelf and he began to play. As the music filled the room the girl looked less afraid, and a bit later she smiled. Eventually, when Magnus offered her some warm milk with bread dipped in it, she ate and seemed to relax.

He spoke to her gently, explaining that the sudden storm and the wash of the waves had taken her out to sea. He told her that she was welcome to stay in his cottage for as long as she wished and he wouldn't bother her in any way.

The following day Magnus went out in his boat and caught many fish. He cooked some of the fish for supper, but the girl ate her share raw. The extra fish that Magnus caught he sold and used the money to buy the girl a pretty dress. She put it on and ran outside the cottage. Magnus lifted his fiddle and, going after her, he began to play. The selkie-girl was skipping on the beach and singing, gentle and sweet, like soft wind over calm water. Magnus heard the pull and drag of the sea on the shingle and saw the creamy crest of the waves as they flowed in towards the sand. The selkie-girl stood with feet tapping and body swaying. As she danced she lifted her skirt to show two dainty feet and she exclaimed at her toes and wriggled them in the sand. Magnus asked her to be his wife and she agreed. He looked into the eyes of the selkie-girl and they were as blue as the sea in summer.

By the time next summer arrived a child was born.

Magnus was delighted at their fine strong son, and the selkie-girl was happy too and she sang lullabies to her baby. But on Midsummer's Eve, as they bathed the child, they noticed that between the baby's big toe and the second toe there was a flap of skin. The selkie-girl examined her own feet. There was a flap of skin between every one of her toes. She glanced at Magnus's feet. All of his toes were separate. The selkie-girl gazed past Magnus through the open door of the cottage where, far out to sea, the heads of seals were bobbing in the water.

Magnus saw her become pale and she whispered, "I miss my own people."

Magnus pointed to the baby and at himself. "*We* are your people now."

The sun, low in the sky, shone upon the water and made it look as if a path of liquid gold was marked out to be followed.

"I must go to them," said the selkie-girl.

A terrible foreboding was in Magnus's heart. He said, "No. I forbid you to go."

"I need my selkie skin," she begged him. "I want to visit my family."

But Magnus only shook his head, for he was worried that she would go away forever.

At that the selkie-girl began to weep. But Magnus remained unmoved, for now he was very afraid. If she went to see her people then she might never return to him. The wind began to blow outside and it carried with it the sound of singing, a selkie song, coming closer as the seals swam in towards the shore. Magnus jumped to his feet and bolted the cottage door. The singing grew louder and the selkie-girl cried out in despair, "They are calling to me."

She stretched her arms out towards the sea and sobs shook her body. And Magnus looked into her eyes and they were as grey as the sea in winter. Magnus knew she was deeply unhappy and because he loved her so much he saw that if he did not let her go her heart would break. So he went to the chest under the bed and he gave his wife her selkie skin.

"Please!" he shouted as the selkie-girl rushed out of the cottage. "Please don't forget me and our child! Please say that you'll come back one day!"

The next night Magnus played his fiddle by the seashore. But no answering song sounded through the air. Eventually, worn out and sorrowful, he went to bed. In the morning when he awoke he found a tiny seashell on the empty pillow beside him. When he went to pick up his child to feed him breakfast, another shell, exactly the same, lay beside the boy's head.

Lifting his son, Magnus went outside. Footprints marked the sand from seashore to cottage and back again where the slim bare feet of a woman had walked. That night and each night thereafter Magnus tried to stay awake to catch a glimpse of his selkie-wife, but always, before dawn, his eyes drooped shut and he fell asleep. Every morning there was a seashell left for him and the child. Sometimes Magnus dreamed as he slept, drifting dreams of half-awakening when he would see his selkie-wife bent over the cradle, quietly crooning to their son. And never once in all that time did the child waken in his sleep or cry out and disturb Magnus in his. As the weeks and months passed, the little boy grew bigger. If the child fretted and wouldn't settle to go to bed at night Magnus carried him to the sea, and the sound of the surf on the rocks of the skerries and the tangy smell of the ocean made the boy smile. His eyes would close and he rested peacefully.

A year passed and Midsummer arrived once more on Sanday. Magnus forced himself to remain awake throughout that night, hoping that he might see his selkie-wife. But although he sat at the door of his cottage and played his fiddle the whole night long, neither seal nor selkie came to the beach.

In the morning Magnus put his son into his harness, strapped him securely on his back, and took his boat out. The sea was choppy but he was determined to go to the skerry where he'd first seen his selkie-wife. When he got there the rock was empty and the waves slapped against the sides of his boat. Tears ran down Magnus's cheeks and they dropped, one by one, into the sea. When this happened the water immediately became still. Then the waves parted and the head of a seal broke through. The dark eyes of the creature fixed themselves upon Magnus. He sighed. It was just another seal – bobbing about his boat looking for something to eat.

Sadly Magnus began to turn the boat to head for shore. Then he noticed the eyes of the seal alter slightly. Magnus blinked. His heart began to beat very fast. He bent his head to look more closely at the seal. As he stared and stared the seal's eyes changed colour from black to stormy grey and then to palest blue.

"Mama!" the child in the boat gurgled and stretched out his arms.

Magnus stretched out his own arms and grasped those of his selkie-wife. And the eyes that looked back at Magnus and the boy were as blue as the sea on a summer's day.

m the greatest bird because I can rise higher in the sky

see further than any other

see the castles of Edinburgh and Balmoral

the tiny wren could never keep up

ook at my magnificent wings

up and up the eagle soared

The Eagle and the Wren

This is a tale from the Western Isles,
the beautiful Hebridean Islands that lie
off the coast of Scotland in the waters
of the Atlantic and whose next-door
neighbour to the west is America.

A mighty eagle and a little wren began to talk one day.

"I am the greatest bird of the skies," the mighty eagle boasted, "and all others must bow down before me."

"What makes you so great," asked the little wren, "that you think other birds should honour you in this way?"

"Look at my magnificent wings," said the mighty eagle. He preened his feathers and spread out his huge wings. "Are these not the widest wings of any bird you have seen?"

"They are very wide indeed," the little wren agreed. "But I don't know if that makes you the greatest bird of all."

"I am the greatest bird because I can rise higher in the sky and see further than any other bird," declared the mighty eagle.

"I am not so sure about that," replied the little wren.

"Are you not, indeed?" The mighty eagle laughed scornfully. "I challenge thee to rise higher in the sky and see further than me."

With a noisy flapping of his wings the mighty eagle took off. He flew round in circles several times to get properly airborne. While the eagle was doing this the little wren flew straight up into the air.

As the mighty eagle rose into the sky he said, "Little wren! Where are you now?"

"Above thee," replied the little wren.

The mighty eagle flapped his wings harder and climbed upwards.

"Little wren," said the mighty eagle, "I can see the Isle of Skye and the Cuillins."

"So can I," said the little wren. "But I see further still. I can also see the Isle of Mull and the Isle of Iona and the Isle of Staffa with the famous cave of Fingal."

The mighty eagle was astonished that such a small bird as the wren could match pace with him in this way. He beat his wings and flew even higher than before. "Now I can see Oban and the Whirlpool of the Corryvreckan," he said.

"So can I," said the little wren. "But I see further still. I can also see Loch Lomond and Glasgow city and Stirling Castle."

Up and up the eagle soared and when he was sure he'd left the wren far below he called out, "Little wren, I can see the castles of Edinburgh and Balmoral."

"So can I," said the little wren. "But I see further still. I can also see Aviemore and Aberdeen and Loch Ness."

The mighty eagle was furious. With a tremendous effort he strained and spread his wings as wide as possible and mounted as high as he could into the sky. He thought that the tiny wren could

never keep up with him now so he shouted in his loudest voice, "I can see from Haddington to the high Highlands."

"So can I," said the little wren. "But I see further still. I can also see from the far Shetlands to the Border country. I see all of Scotland."

"I don't understand," said the mighty eagle. "I am the greatest bird of the air and king of the skies yet I cannot rise any higher or see further than I do now."

"But I will always be able to see more than you," said the little wren.

"How can that be?" the mighty eagle asked.

And the little wren replied, "Oh mighty eagle, I am higher in the sky and can see further, for I am nestled among your feathers on your back here above thee."

granny told them stories every night before going to bed

in the wild places and the not so wild places

a terrible accident on the cro

a wizened little figure

almost as broad as he was tall

an churn and cook and clean

The Brownie of Ballharn Hill

There are lots of stories about brownies in the folklore of Scotland; some of them are very scary indeed! Traditional tales show the brownie to be like a goblin or an elf who works hard but hides himself away due to his shyness and strange appearance. He seeks out a family in need and when they are asleep he does the chores and helps in any way he can. It's said that the only reward he wants is food and milk. If any other kind of payment is offered he will be offended and is liable to leave. This story is similar to the one about the cobbler's elves. I think it was told to me by my parents to let me know that being helpful around the house should not always require payment!

There was once a girl and a boy named Fiona and Finn.

Fiona and Finn were sister and brother, and if I tell you that not only were they brother and sister, but they were exactly the same age then I guess you would tell me that they were twins. And you would be right!

They had been orphaned when they were very young and now they lived with their granny in a small croft in the very north of Scotland – the bit that looks like the top of a witch's hat.

Fiona and Finn were content to live with their granny. Although she made them learn their lessons and clean their teeth twice a day and wash their hands before eating, she kept them well fed with bowls of porridge and fresh fish and clootie dumplings.

The reason that Fiona and Finn's granny could keep them so well fed was because they lived on land near a river. There was a meadow where their cow and sheep could graze, a field where they grew their crops, fruit trees and the river where they caught fish when they had a mind to. And so the twins bided happily in the croft for, as well as feeding them, their granny told them stories every night before going to bed.

Some of the twins' favourite stories were about the Brownie of Ballharn Hill. Ballharn Hill was close to the croft and also to the place of the stones known as the Grey Cairns of Camster. Their granny said that these ancient stones held the old magic of long, long ago and that a very special creature known as a brownie lived there from time to time. But, their granny told them, they would never see the Brownie of Ballharn Hill for not only was he very shy, he usually was out and about doing what brownies do; that is, looking after those in need.

The brownie who lived in Ballharn Hill did indeed go about the north of Scotland – in the wild places and the not so wild places – helping folks, but now and then he came home to rest at Ballharn Hill. And as this story takes place then *and* now, it happened that one of the times when the brownie was coming home to Ballharn Hill there was a terrible accident on the croft.

Winter was over so Fiona and Finn's granny started spring cleaning. She got onto the kitchen table to dust the top of a high cupboard, but she couldn't quite stretch far enough. Looking round the kitchen she spotted a stool by the fire and decided to put this stool on top of the table. Up she clambered, first onto the table, and then onto the stool on top of the table.

Crash!

The twins rushed in from playing outside to find Granny in a heap on the floor.

"Och! Och! Och!" Granny cried in pain. "I've braikit ma leg for sure! Send for the doctor!"

The doctor came and declared Granny's leg to be broken and said that she must rest it for at least three months.

"Och, this is a disaster," said Granny when the doctor had gone. "Who will milk the kye and churn the butter?"

"Why, I can do that," said Finn.

"Who will gaither the wool and spin it into yarn?"

"Why, I can do that," said Fiona.

"Who will cook the food and clean the hoose?"

"Why, we can both do that," said Fiona and Finn together.

"Who will plough the field and mak it ready to plant the crops?"

The twins looked at each other and didn't say anything, for they knew that neither of them was strong enough to plough the field.

"Ye ken if that's no done there will be nae food for winter," said the twins' granny, and she threw her apron over her head and fell to weeping and wailing.

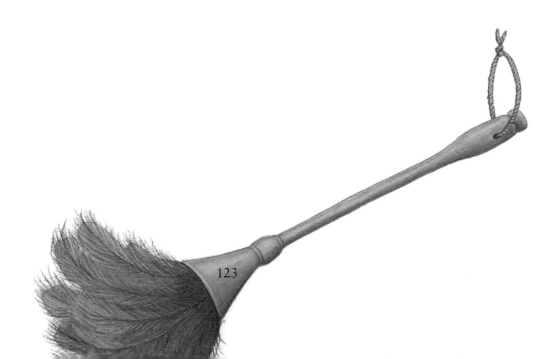

Fiona and Finn were very upset and they went outside the croft to think what they might do. And it just so happened that the Brownie of Ballharn Hill was passing on his way home when he heard the twins' conversation. Now a good brownie can never ignore a cry for help and the Brownie of Ballharn Hill was a very good brownie, and he felt sorry for the twins and their granny.

He hid behind the hedge and he sang a song:

I can plough a field for planting,
I can spin the wool forbye,
I can churn and cook and clean
And I can milk the kye.

The twins stopped talking to listen to this strange song. They ran round to the other side of the hedge to see who was there. But as soon as they did that the brownie jumped into a ditch and covered himself with leaves so that he wouldn't be seen. Fiona and Finn searched about but they couldn't find the singer of the song. When it was getting dark they went inside the croft and told their granny what had happened.

"It might be the Brownie of Ballharn Hill," Granny said at once. "Ye maun mak a bannock and spread it with heather honey and

place it beside the stool by the fire with a bowl of cream. If it's gone in the morning we'll ken that the brownie has come to live with us and help us in our hour of need."

Fiona and Finn did as their granny told them and the next day when they got up the food and drink were gone! When Fiona and Finn went to the byre the cow had been milked. When they went to the churn it was full of butter. When they went to the field one furrow had been ploughed.

And so it went on. Through springtime the work of the croft was done by the brownie during the hours of darkness. The field was ploughed and planted, the house was cleaned, food was cooked and fish caught. Every night Fiona and Finn left out a bowl of cream and a bannock spread with heather honey, and in the morning there was not a bannock crumb nor a lick of cream left.

In summer the crops grew and the fruit ripened. Then the wind shifted round and the leaves on the trees began to turn russet and gold. It was the harvest season. Fruit was collected in baskets, potatoes dug up, grain threshed and fish salted and cured. All was stored ready for the winter. During this time Fiona and Finn became more and more curious about the brownie. One night they resolved to stay awake in the hope that they might see him. They set out the food as usual on the stool by the fire but, instead of going to bed, they hid in the kitchen cupboard and peeked out through a crack in the door.

On the stroke of midnight the outside door opened and a strange creature entered the croft. He was a wizened little figure, almost as broad as he was tall, with long hair and beard. His arms hung down to the floor and he was dressed only in a short kilt made from green bracken.

As he came into the kitchen he was singing a song:

Fresh cream and heather honey
They leave out as my treat.
I'll eat the bonnie bannock
While I warm my feet!

The children knew to remain very quiet so as not to frighten the brownie, but as soon as he'd finished his supper and gone off to do his work Fiona whispered, "No wonder he's cold. Apart from a little kilt made of green bracken wrapped round his waist the brownie is bare-naked!"

"He has no shoes," Finn whispered back. "His feet must hurt when he walks upon the rocks."

The next morning Fiona and Finn went to the chest where their granny kept her dressmaking materials. They took out leather and good cloth and told their granny that they wanted to make the brownie some clothes and shoes.

"Ye never leave a brownie anything except food and drink," said their granny.

"He needs clothes," the twins replied. "He's only got a green bracken kilt and no shoes upon his feet."

"I warn ye now," said their granny. "If ye give him a gift ye'll see nae brownie in his bracken kilt again."

"But we are older now and strong enough to do more around the croft," said Fiona.

"And winter is coming," added Finn. "If the brownie has no cloak or shoes then he will suffer from the cold."

The twins' granny looked at them and she felt very proud of Fiona and Finn for their willingness to help and their kind thoughts. She knew also that very soon her leg would be completely mended and good as new and perhaps it was time for the brownie to depart.

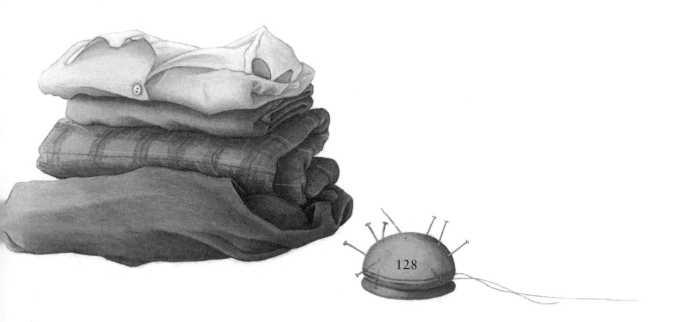

So she gave the twins cloth and leather and showed them how to cut and stitch and sew. Fiona and Finn worked hard and made the brownie a little suit. It had a shirt of yellow, a green waistcoat, tartan trousers and shoes of red leather. And to wear over all of this was a fine cloak of worsted wool with a bright blue hood.

A few days later, as well as setting out a bowl of cream and the bannock spread with heather honey, Fiona and Finn laid the clothes and shoes they'd made on the stool by the fire. When they got up the next day the suit was gone, but so was the Brownie of Ballharn Hill. They watched him leave, and he sang as he walked on up the road:

I've a new waistcoat and red leather shoes,
A smart yellow shirt and long tartan trews,
I've a fine woollen cloak with a bright blue hood,
I'm off somewhere else where I'll do most good.

The twins' granny said, "Aye, I told ye. Ye don't pay a brownie with anything other than food else he takes offence."

"I don't think the brownie was offended," said Finn.

"Nor me either," said Fiona. "I think he saw that your leg was better and we no longer needed him. So he has moved on to help someone who does."

And then the twins asked their granny a question that she could not answer: "If the brownie was so offended, why did he put on the clothes and take them away with him?"

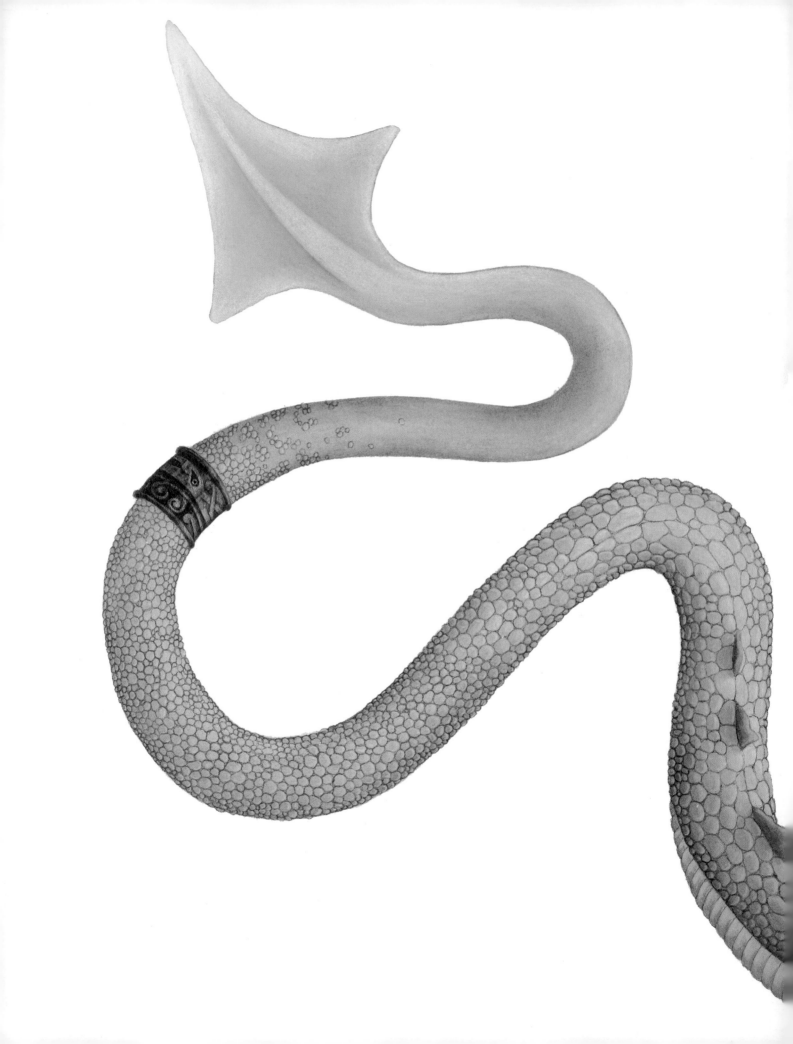

The Dragon Stoorworm and the Boy Called Assipattle

There are quite a few stories about the boy known as Assipattle. He was the seventh son of a seventh son and a bit of a dreamer. While his father and brothers worked hard, Assipattle was more content to sit at the hearth and make up poems and stories. He was often berated for being lazy and useless, but when things went wrong it was Assipattle, with his quick wits, who was able to overcome any problems and be the hero of the story.

This is the story of the Dragon Stoorworm

– the very first, and the very worst, dragon ever to exist from the beginning of time. Compared to the Dragon Stoorworm, all other dragons are teeny-tiny namby-pamby kinds of dragons who couldn't frighten a baby, let alone a whole country. And the Dragon Stoorworm *did* frighten a whole country when it decided to take up residence there, and in this story that country was Scotland.

The first scary thing about the Dragon Stoorworm was its size. It was absolutely gi*nor*mous. The Stoorworm was so vast that it almost completely covered Scotland, from the very top to the very bottom, and all the way across from side to side. It wouldn't have been such a problem for Scotland when the Stoorworm arrived if it had been a friendly sort of dragon – you know, the type that greets you with a pleasant "good morning" or "good afternoon" and enquires how things are with you and asks after the health of your granny – then its enormous size wouldn't have been so worrying. But if the Dragon Stoorworm enquired as to the whereabouts of your granny, or indeed any of your relatives, it was because it intended to eat them. And if you tried to avoid telling it or hesitated to reply, then it'd most likely gobble you up instead.

The second scary thing about the Dragon Stoorworm was its enormous tail, which had jaggy spikes along it. When it was in a bad mood (which was often) the Stoorworm lashed this tail about, causing a considerable amount of damage. Churches, houses, whole villages, and even a mountain or two, were crushed and swept away.

The third scary thing about the Dragon Stoorworm was its eating habits. The Stoorworm would open its mouth and swallow cows, horses, sheep, ducks, geese and any other livestock that it spotted. Quite often it liked to toast these first. Long flickers of flame would shoot out of its mouth, scorching anybody who happened to be passing by, and setting ablaze thatched roofs of cottages and most of the surrounding fields as well.

Before long, Scotland was in a bad way. There were no crops growing (they'd all been burned by the Stoorworm), there was little livestock (eaten by the Stoorworm), and soon there would be no fresh water, for every morning when the Stoorworm woke up it opened its huge mouth and yawned, swallowing gallons of water from the loch where it was resting its gigantic head.

The king sent his three wisest men to talk to the Dragon Stoorworm and to ask it to stop causing so much trouble and to suggest that it might like to go away and visit a different country. The Stoorworm ate two of the wise men, but the third managed to run very fast and escape. He came back with a message to say that the Stoorworm would stop destroying villages, guzzling cattle and incinerating crops if the king sent it a pretty girl that it could eat for breakfast each morning.

As soon as the menfolk heard this they hurried to lock up their daughters and wives and sisters. But the womenfolk, who weren't slow to catch on and not minded to hang about, had already gone and hidden themselves.

The only girl that was left was the king's own daughter, the Princess Gemdelovely. Now the Princess Gemdelovely was brave and good, and she said that she would go and sacrifice herself if it would help to stop the Dragon Stoorworm from ruining the whole country.

The king, her father, was very upset when she came to say goodbye to him. He held up his famous sword, Sickersnapper, and cried out that he'd give his sword, his kingdom and the hand of his daughter in marriage to anyone who could free Scotland of the Stoorworm. To which the Princess Gemdelovely replied that her father could do what he liked with his kingdom and his sword, but as far as she was concerned her hands belonged to her and she'd marry whom she pleased. And she went to sit in the tower of the castle to wait and see who would turn up to slay the Stoorworm.

Many warriors from here and there, and this land and that, came riding up to the castle in the hope of gaining a kingdom, a sword and a princess to marry. Princess Gemdelovely, who always secretly listened when her father was negotiating terms, noted that these men listed the rewards for their work in that order: the kingdom, the sword, the princess. She was *always* last and frequently they didn't even ask her name!

From her seat in the tower Princess Gemdelovely inspected the knights, nobles and commoners as they rode out in turn each morning to do battle with the Dragon Stoorworm. They never came back and no trace of them was ever found – well, perhaps just an occasional stirrup or a plume feather from a knight's helmet: things that got stuck in the throat of the Dragon Stoorworm and were spat out on the side of the loch. Although the Princess Gemdelovely was sad that the warriors perished, none of them had touched her heart until one day a boy called Assipattle wandered along the road.

Assipattle was the seventh son of a seventh son and as such was a bit different from most boys. Instead of rushing about fighting and playing noisy games, he liked to sing and sit by the fire to read and think and make up poems, stories and songs. This had got him into bother with his parents and brothers, who shouted at him all the time to move himself and do what they considered real work.

"Assipattle, can you not help milk the kye?" his mother would say.

To which Assipattle would reply, "I've just made up a beautiful poem about the kye walking home in the gloaming. Would you like to hear it?"

"Assipattle, can you not help plough the fields?" his father would ask.

To which Assipattle would reply, "There's a song I've written about a ploughman and his horse. Would you like me to sing it to you?"

"Assipattle! Come and help us plant the crops or we will beat your bones," his older brothers shouted at him.

To which Assipattle was about to reply, saying, "I know a story about sowing and reaping. Would you like me to tell it to you?" But looking at the faces of his brothers he realised that they would indeed beat his bones, so Assipattle jumped up from the hearth and went off to find his fortune.

And so, early on a fine morning Assipattle arrived, singing, on the road to the castle. From her tower the Princess Gemdelovely looked down and thought, "Aha... this one looks interesting."

And Assipattle glanced up and he caught sight of the Princess Gemdelovely and he thought, "Aha..."

When Assipattle knocked on the castle door he was taken at once to the king. Now the king was in a desperate state. It was nearly breakfast-time and no more volunteers had arrived to try to slay the Stoorworm. The king was beginning to think that he might have to strap on his mighty sword, Sickersnapper, and go and fight the dragon himself, when a servant announced that someone wanted to speak to him. On seeing Assipattle the king's heart sank right down into his blue slippers. The boy was short and slight and covered in a layer of dusty peat ash from sitting at the fireside and, what's more, had neither horse, nor armour, nor lance, nor mace, nor sword.

"How will you fight the Dragon Stoorworm?" the king asked.

"Oh, I didn't stop by to fight the Dragon Stoorworm," replied Assipattle. "I was passing on the road and saw a girl in your tower and I thought her pretty enough. She'd an honest look about her and I wanted to meet her to talk and share my poems and stories."

Princess Gemdelovely, who was secretly listening as usual, didn't know quite how to react to these words. "Pretty enough!" Pretty *enough*? She was considered stunningly attractive – everyone told her so (although it crossed her mind now that she should perhaps check as soon as she'd a chance to find a mirror). That remark annoyed her, but she did like the fact that this boy thought she'd an honest look and, even though he wasn't aware she was a princess, he wanted to speak with her and share stories.

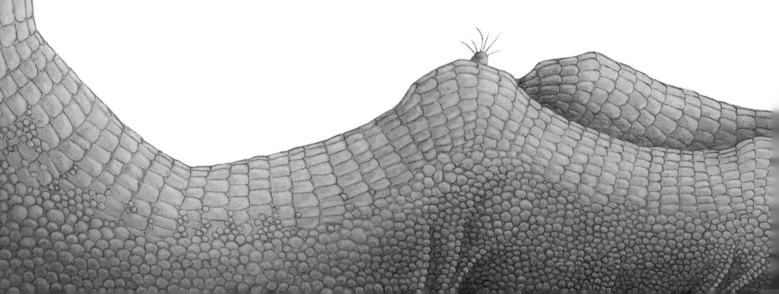

Before her father could reply, Princess Gemdelovely stepped from behind the curtain and said, "Well, now you've met me what do you think? Do you still want to talk to me?"

"I do indeed," said Assipattle and he went forward and held out his hand.

Princess Gemdelovely saw that Assipattle's hand was smudged with peat ash. Nevertheless she took it in her own.

"Hold on a minute," said the king. "There's the matter of the Dragon Stoorworm to be dealt with first." And he explained the situation to Assipattle.

"That's a bit inconvenient," said Assipattle, keeping hold of Princess Gemdelovely's hand.

"I agree," said Princess Gemdelovely, not letting go of the hand of Assipattle.

"Would it be best to get rid of the Dragon Stoorworm before we sat down to chat?" Assipattle suggested.

"It would be very helpful," said Princess Gemdelovely, "otherwise I would have to break off our conversation to go and be breakfast for the Stoorworm."

The king told Assipattle about the three rewards, to which Assipattle replied,

"I have no wish to be a king for I fear it would get in the way of my storytelling. I have no wish to own your sword,

Sickersnapper, for I might be tempted to kill with it, and if I did that it might also kill my own spirit." Assipattle paused and looked at Princess Gemdelovely, and then said, "I *would* like to get to know your daughter but it's really up to us to decide whether we get married or not."

Princess Gemdelovely smiled at Assipattle and they went off together to make a plan to defeat the Dragon Stoorworm.

Each morning when the Dragon Stoorworm awoke, it would yawn mightily and take in a great drink of water from the loch. That morning as the water rushed into the Stoorworm's mouth a tiny boat holding Assipattle and Princess Gemdelovely was also swept inside. They rowed as fast as they were able and their boat was carried past the sharp teeth, over the dreadful tongue and down the throat of the monster. They hung on as the boat was battered from side to side until finally, bumping about, they arrived at the Stoorworm's liver. Princess Gemdelovely held the boat steady as Assipattle took a knife and dug a hole in the flesh of the Stoorworm. Then Princess Gemdelovely opened a jar containing a glowing peat that they'd taken from the fire in the castle. They blew on the peat, not once, not twice, but three times, to make it blaze like a live coal. Then they rammed the peat deep into the liver of the Stoorworm. When they'd done that, Princess Gemdelovely and Assipattle clung together and waited.

Very soon the fire from the peat began to hurt the Dragon Stoorworm. As it got hotter and hotter the Stoorworm started to writhe and moan. The more its liver was burning the more it howled in torment. It screeched and screamed, and screamed and screeched. Groaning in agony, it tried to get rid of the pain in its belly by gagging and spewing. And so the Stoorworm vomited the boat, with Princess Gemdelovely and Assipattle in it, out of its mouth and back into the waters of the loch.

As the little boat heaved about, Assipattle stood up. Princess Gemdelovely handed him the king's sword, Sickersnapper, and Assipattle skelped the Dragon Stoorworm the most tremendous blow on the side of its head. Assipattle struck with such force that the Stoorworm was sent rocketing into the sky and was knocked out cold for ten thousand years and a day.

Assipattle kissed Princess Gemdelovely three times and asked if she'd marry him. The Princess Gemdelovely kissed Assipattle seven times and decided that she would. And so they lived long and happily together in the land of Scotland.

"And did the Dragon Stoorworm ever return?" I hear you ask.

Well, Assipattle gave the Dragon Stoorworm's head such a clatter with the king's sword that the Stoorworm's tongue and eyes and teeth flew out. The tongue went east and landed between Scotland and Norway, two countries which were at that time joined together. It crashed to earth with a thump so hard that Scotland and Norway split apart and so created the North Sea.

The Stoorworm's eyes popped out and they went west. Spinning round and round, they plummeted deep into the stretch of water between Jura and Scarba. They continue to spin there to this very day, and that place is known as the Whirlpool of the Corryvreckan.

One by one the shattered teeth of the Stoorworm splashed down around Scotland and formed isles and islets and skerries. There are many of these, including the beautiful Shetland Islands.

The whole of the Stoorworm's body went north, landing with a terrific thud near the top of the world. The sea hissed and boiled for a while but then the cold Arctic Ocean froze around and over it and the great lump became the country called Iceland.

He lies there still, the Dragon Stoorworm, deep below the snow and ice. But every so often when he is disturbed he opens his mouth and a great belch of smoke and fire erupts from the earth and flames leap high into the sky. Some folk call these volcanoes, but it is really the Dragon Stoorworm snoring in his sleep.

if you would only let me hold on to the end of your long plait

uld take her home and gobble her up for supper

the wily fox closed his eye

he was just an ordinary girl, who lived in an ordinary house with ordinary parents

Tale End

I have visited many countries of the world and there
is a version of this story in every one. It's often used
by storytellers to end a session or, as in this case,
to be the final story in a book.

There was once a girl called Kirsty MacLeod.

She was just an ordinary girl, who lived in an ordinary house with ordinary parents. Kirsty had long red hair and every morning Kirsty's father would brush out Kirsty's long red hair and Kirsty's mother would pleat it into one single plait that hung down her back.

One day when Kirsty was out walking she came to a bridge over a river. She began to cross the bridge when she saw a wily fox standing in the middle.

The wily fox saw Kirsty and he thought to himself, "That little girl looks good to eat. I could take her home and gobble her up for supper."

So when Kirsty reached the middle of the bridge the fox stopped her and said,

"Hello, little girl."

"Hello, fox," said Kirsty, for she was a polite child and had been taught good manners.

"And where are you off to today?" asked the wily fox.

"That is of no interest to you," Kirsty replied at once, for although she was well mannered she knew that her business was her own and nobody else's.

"You could come and visit me in my den," suggested the wily fox.

"No, thank you," Kirsty replied firmly.

"I have darling baby cubs that you could play with," said the wily fox.

"No!" said Kirsty in a very loud voice.

The wily fox was cross when he saw that this little girl wouldn't do as he asked and so he thought to trap her by a cunning trick.

"I am so sad that I might not see my cubs again," he told Kirsty, "for I am afraid of running water and I cannot go over a river by myself even on this bridge. If you would only let me hold on to the end of your long plait of red hair then I would be able to get across."

Kirsty saw that she would have to think
carefully how best to deal with this wily fox.

"All right," she agreed. "But first you must shut your eyes so that you do not see the running water. Then I will give you the end of my plait to hold."

The wily fox closed his eyes and thought that once he had a grip of Kirsty's plait of hair then he would never let go. He decided he'd pull on it and drag her off to his den and she wouldn't be able to escape.

When she was sure the wily fox's eyes were properly closed, Kirsty took the end of the fox's own long tail and gave it to him to hold.

Of course the wily fox cheated and opened his eyes a tiny bit. But when he saw red hair he thought that he did indeed have the end of Kirsty's long plait between his teeth.

"There," said Kirsty. "Now hold on tight."

"Oh, I will," said the fox. "I certainly will!"

And he pulled as hard as he could. That wily fox pulled and he pulled and he pulled. He pulled so hard that his tail broke off!

"What happened?" screeched the fox. He opened his eyes and began to howl in pain.

"Why," said wily Kirsty as she ran off home, "you've reached the end of your tail!"

"And so have I," said Theresa Breslin,
"I have reached the end of all my tales."

n the greatest bird because I can rise higher in the sky

idled away his days in doing as little as possible

baby boy as he dribbled and drobbled goo over his clothes

eals swam in towards the shore

selkies would dance and sin

Glossary

A

Assipattle: The "Ass" in Assipattle comes from an Orcadian word for "ashes" and the word "pattle" originally meant "to dabble or sit among". So the name "Assipattle" has a meaning like "Cinder Boy" – somewhat similar to a male Cinderella.

B

bannock: a kind of pancake made mainly from oatmeal.

bide: live, to stay, remain. Can also mean delay, wait, as in, "bide your time".

bier: platform on which a coffin or a body rests before burial.

blether: to boast or talk foolishly or too much.

boon: a favour – to ask for a boon is to make a request for something.

bonny, bonnie: good-looking, handsome, pretty.

Borders, The: The land around the border between Scotland and England – also known as the Debatable Lands.

braikit: broken.

brand: a piece of burning wood, torch.

brownie: a small strange magical creature who will move in with a family in need and do chores for them.

byre: cowshed.

C

clippit: to cut, trim.

clootie: a cloth.

clootie dumpling: a traditional Scottish fruit pudding made with flour, breadcrumbs, currants, suet, syrup, sugar and spices mixed together then wrapped in a cloth and boiled.

croft: a small farm.

cur: a worthless or snappy dog.

D

drover: a person who drives cattle or sheep to market, sometimes over very many miles.

F

forbye: in addition, as well as.

G

gaither: gather.

glen: a valley.

gloaming: twilight or dusk.

goshawk: a large hawk, used in falconry.

gowd(en): gold(en).

guid-wife: goodwife, wife, or woman of the house.

guid-man: goodman, husband, or man of the house.

guinea: twenty-one shillings in old money, one pound and ten pence today.

H

hame: home.

hap(ped): to wrap up (wrapped up).

hen-wife: an older woman who looked after the hens and poultry on large farms or estates and was thought to be wise in the ways of the world.

hoose: house.

K

keep: a fortified tower, like a small castle.

kelpie: The name "kelpie" is said to come from the Gaelic word *colpach* – a colt. In Scottish folklore the kelpie is a malign spirit that lives near rivers and lochs, and takes the form of a horse that tries to drown anyone who rides it.

ken: know.

kye: cow.

L

lass(ie): a young girl.

last: a cobbler's model of wood or metal, which is used for making or repair-ing a shoe or boot.

list: listen.

loch: a lake, can be inland or a sea loch (but kelpies are said not to like salt water).

M

ma: my. Can also mean mother.

mak: make.

mantelshelf: a shelf above a fireplace.

maun: must.

N

nae / nay: no.

nippit: tight-fitting (usually clothes or shoes).

no: not.

O

och: expression of pain, regret, annoyance or weariness.

P

plaid(ie): a large piece of cloth usually of woven and heavy material used like a shawl. Highlanders used to sleep with plaids wrapped round their bodies and this eventually became the modern-day kilt.

R

rashie: rush – a plant that grows in wet places and can be woven to make mats, baskets etc or in this story a cheap coat.

reivers: border people who raided farms and villages, stealing from those who lived there.

S

score: twenty.

selkie: the word for "seal" from Orcadian – the language of the Orkney Islands.

shilling: old money, replaced by the five-pence coin.

skelp(ed): to slap or strike (slapped, struck).

skerry (skerries): small rocky island(s).

shoon: shoes.

spae-wife: a wise woman or a woman who can foretell the future.

Stoorworm: In old legends the word "worm" was used to describe a dragon or a huge sea serpent, and "stoor" can mean large and/or violent. There are lots of versions of the story about the first and worst dragon ever to roam the earth. When I was young I was told that the one I have included here came from the Shetland Islands.

stourie: a light-footed, nimble person.

T

tartan: multi-coloured design of straight lines arranged to make a chequered appearance – each Scottish clan or family has its own design.

thee: you.

thon: that.

thy (thine): your(s).

trews: trousers.

W

wee: small.

Wee Folk or Other People: The name given in Scotland to the fairy folk. They were thought to dress in green when they took human form, and sometimes they tried to be cruel to humans.

Y

ye: you.

Theresa Breslin

Theresa Breslin is a highly acclaimed,
Carnegie Medal-winning author, who has published
over thirty books for children and young adults. She
lives near Glasgow, Scotland. Her work has been filmed
for television, broadcast on radio and translated into
many languages. Theresa worked as a librarian before
becoming a full-time writer; she is passionate about
children's literature and literacy.

Kate Leiper

Kate Leiper is an artist and illustrator
based in Edinburgh, Scotland. She studied at Gray's
School of Art in Aberdeen, and her work has been
exhibited in galleries from London to the north of
Scotland. She has been commissioned for projects by
the Scottish Storytelling Centre and the Royal Lyceum
Theatre. Inspirations for her work range from Scottish
folklore, to tales from the Far East, to Shakespeare.

An Illustrated
Treasury of
**Scottish
Mythical
Creatures**

Theresa Breslin Kate Leiper

'This is a rare delight; a harmonious braiding of pitch-perfect
storytelling with illustrations of breathtaking elegance and integrity.
Every home should have at least one copy.'

DEBI GLIORI

'Theresa Breslin brings an array of creatures to life with her assured and
captivating storytelling, and she places a child at the heart of each tale.'

JULIA DONALDSON

florisbooks.co.uk